DUSK OVER THE MUSTARD FIELDS

Dusk over the Mustard Fields

Ranjit Powar

THE BR◆WSER

www.thebrowser.org

Publishers & Booksellers

First Published in India by **The Browser** 2020
(An imprint of J.G.S. Enterprises Pvt. Ltd.)
SCO 14-15, Sector 8-C, Chandigarh 160 009
Email: service@thebrowser.org

www.thebrowser.org

Dedicated to:

My father Lt. Col. Daljeet Singh,
who recreated the ethos of the British
Indian Army for me, and my mother Har-
sharan Kaur, my greatest resource for
Punjabi history and culture.

CONTENTS

A Note for the Reader

In a period novel and a culture-specific one at that, the modern reader may come across many unfamiliar words needing an explanation. The glossary at the end introduces the reader to some typical, delightful Punjabi expressions.

1

Portrait of a Punjabi Village

Deep in the dry sandy stretches of the Malwa region, in pre-partition Punjab, there lay the sprawling village of Sahnewal—its skyline a mixture of high havelis and humble mud houses surrounded by acres of green fields and groves of dark, thorny keekar and neem. A rivulet that flowed to the south fed the thirsty fields with a network of drains spread like veins in a body. The tall 'Nishan Sahib' of the gurudwara soaring into the sky and the green minarets of a mosque were visible from afar. The entrance to the village was through a huge arched deori made artistically from small Nanakshahi bricks. It mourned a majestic past but was now a crumbly structure surrounded by little mounds of dislocated bricks that the village children played with. The deori morphed into an elongated covered passage with broad raised platforms on the inner sides for weary travellers to sit on. These were mostly claimed by mangy stray dogs and runny-nosed urchins in loose undershorts, except when they were shooed off by the village addicts and vagabonds who would then sit for hours over a game of cards or dice. Scratchy bitches nursed their litters and waited expectantly for scraps of food from passersby. Sometimes a wandering Muslim fakir in black robes or a Hindu mendicant in an ochre wrap camped there for a day or two, hoping for some alms from the villagers.

A narrow brick-paved lane led into the inner village, winding through small dung heaps, dried dung cakes and flat-roofed mud huts of communities like the chamar, nai, julaha and luhar. On the eastern edge of the village stood a mosque containing the Qibla, a Mehrab in the wall indicating the direction towards Mecca which the faithful faced while praying. The northern side had a large, placid pond covered with green algae and lotus, ringed with keekar trees and tall reeds. Each morning buffaloes from the village households were brought to bathe in the pond by scrawny young boys in striped shorts who rode on their shiny black backs and splashed water on each other.

A little away from the pond was the mazar of Peer Murad Shah, a Sufi faqeer said to have lived and died there. It stood sheltered under the benevolent shade of a huge pipal tree, with a soot-blackened brick alcove where barren women and desperate ageing bachelors lit small earthen lamps on Friday. The mazar was open to applications from all with unfulfilled secret wishes—Sikh, Muslim, and Hindu. In the fields, Persian wheels squeaked and groaned while their moving chain of tin water troughs made a clinking noise. The troughs rotated to dip deep into the well, scoop-up water and empty it into a drain leading to the fields. Pairs of oxen with blinkers on their eyes made endless rounds of the wells, prodded with sticks and juicy references to their sisters by urchins riding on the long wooden arms attached to the giant Persian wheels. It all created a piece of sonorous, rhythmic music. Groves of neem trees shaded the wells which had water tanks for bathing and washing clothes.

A large daera in the center of the village had a common well from which the women drew water for their daily needs and met to exchange the latest village gossip. Did the Kumhars' buffalo have a female or a male calf? Lala Bhairo's son-in-law came to visit yesterday but did not take his wife along. Nindi's mother-in-law coughed through the night; Waheguru alone knows how many more breaths she has left in her. Chhinda got drunk and beat his wife again last night; one could hear her screams ten houses away. The lower castes, of course, weren't permitted to draw water here and had their small well on the periphery of the village. There was also a large pipal tree in the daera with a raised platform around it, which afforded a club area for the older men to sit and chat and the younger ones to play cards. Women were mindful of drawing a veil over their faces when passing by the assembled men.

The social set up of Sahnewal was interwoven and interdependent with all three communities playing their special role in its economy—the population being a mix of Sikhs, Hindus and some Muslims. The major landholdings were held by Sikhs and some Muslim Jats, while the Hindus controlled various businesses. The majority of workers and artisans were Muslim. There was both a

Muslim Yunani hakim and a Hindu vaid, but religion was the last thing ailing people had on their minds. Any Muslim who had travelled to Mecca and Medina was a Haji or Hajjan and revered by all. The few Brahmin families made a living by performing priestly functions on special socio-religious occasions like births, weddings and deaths, but did not enjoy much status or privileges. Major festivals of all religions were celebrated collectively. Baisakhi meant celebrating the harvesting of crops for all, while every house lighted lamps on Diwali and joined Eid festivities.

People generously gave alms of jaggery or flour to Muslim fakirs and Hindu mendicants who came to their door. Most houses put aside a couple of rotis each day to give to the boys who came to collect them for the gurudwara and the mandir. The Singh Sabha movement and the Arya Samaj had yet to make an impact in the area. People had simple, innocent beliefs—their everyday problems like drying up of a buffalo's milk or a wayward son would be solved by making offerings and praying to any of the different Gods or at the mazar of Peer Murad Shah by the village pond. There was, till then, not much of a sense of proprietorship over Gods. The long drawn out notes of the muezzin's azaan from the mosque, the lilting notes of the Japji Sahib paath from the Gurudwara, and the melodious jingle of the mandir bells ushered in the dawn in the village. Communal disturbances that had started in some cities in Punjab had not yet percolated down to the villages. No one thought they would.

Pukka havelis of the village elite surrounded the daera. The tallest one belonged to the largest landowning jagirdar, Zaildar Kehar Singh, while adjacent ones belonged to the village moneylender, Lala Beli Shah and the horse breeder Mian Ali Beg.

The havelis were typically double-storied, built with Nanakshahi bricks, with beautiful stained-glass windows and decorative awnings. Zaildar Kehar Singh was in charge of five villages for law-and-order and was frequently called upon to intervene for settling quarrels between feuding parties. The Zaildar's haveli stood the grandest of all, built by Kehar Singh's grandfather and carrying an inscription in Gurumukhi above the gate: "Nahar Singh Niwas, Year 1880".

On the outer side in the street, the entrance was flanked by two smaller raised platforms built under decorative jharokhas. The roof of the portico was an arched, half canopy resting on delicately carved pillars, decorated with brightly painted, embossed floral stucco work, now partially faded after withstanding half-a-century of scorching summers and sandstorms. Brass studded, finely carved wooden doors opened into the brick-paved street and stood ajar to welcome visitors. The Zaildar loved to narrate how his grandfather had summoned master craftsmen from Peshawar to carve those doors.

The passage inside was flanked by baithaks, their walls painted with scenes from Hindu and Sikh mythology. Beyond these was a large inner courtyard with rooms and verandas on three sides, and stairs leading up to the next level. An old neem tree with a dark, gnarled trunk stood in one corner, its long branches drooping down to shade an open kitchen cordoned off with a three feet high mud wall. A row of mud chullahs and an oven sat inside the right wall of this kitchen, a pile of dry cotton-plant branches and cow dung patties piled next to them for fuel. A couple of jute manjis lay strewn in the courtyard along with some peerhis woven in navy and red-coloured cotton string for the women to sit on. In the veranda stood a canvas deck chair in which the Zaildar sahib liked to sit and read his daily newspapers—Milap, Veer Bharat, and Zamindar. The women spent most of the day in the courtyard, basking in the luxurious warmth of the sun in winter, spinning, weaving, cleaning mustard leaves for saag, oiling and combing out children's hair, and discussing births and marriages. A mean-looking, white and black hound with a wasp waist stretched out under the chequered shade of a manji, lifting its ears and growling at the sound of any unfamiliar footsteps.

Zaildar Kehar Singh's family consisted of his wife Chinti, two daughters Nimmo and Bholan, his mother and Nama, his younger brother. Nama was held to be mentally unsound as his moods swung between extreme withdrawal and occasional hysteria. The Zaildar's mother was a tall, majestic, wiry woman who ruled over the household with an iron hand, and her son seldom challenged her decisions. She was Maji to all, and the children probably were not even aware that she had a given name. Maji had taken to wearing white mulmul dupattas ever since she lost her husband but was very particular that her clothes were always spotlessly clean and well turned out. She wore the coolest 'lawn' cotton which came from Lahore, and juttis made from the softest kid leather which could fold round all the way.

Maji felt cheated by fate that her younger son could not be married due to his disability, while Kehar Singh had only daughters. She would be the first one to wake up before sunrise each morning, take a bath after drawing water from the well and recite her Japji loudly enough to nudge awake anyone who still snored. She held a grudge against her daughter-in-law Chinti for not producing a male heir and tried to urge Kehar Singh to take a second wife. But being a man of some wisdom and maturity, he ignored her proposals. Chinti and her daughters often bore the brunt of Maji's anger for being deprived of a grandson. Whenever she chastised the girls for any lapse, she would refer to the unpardonable sin of their gender.

Nimmo had led a sheltered and uneventful life in her village, not having progressed beyond Gurumukhi and Urdu primers. She was a bright girl, but the nearest school for girls was five miles away in the large village of Narangwal, and it was not the tradition for girls to be sent that far. She was quite happy growing up learning to weave, embroider and cook like most other girls of her age, who were taught enough to be able to read the Gurbani paath and do basic arithmetic. Who wanted them to read books and newspapers and corrupt their minds?

"Where have both you witches come from to suck my son's blood? Didn't you find another house to go to? The poor man can hardly get enough sleep worrying about your marriages! And look at you, romping and skipping around with not a care in the world."

The girls never took any offence to her remarks, taking it all in their stride. They would hurry to finish the household tasks assigned to them and slip away to play stapu or geete with their friends Tippi, Baggi and Mian Ali Beg's daughters Sakina and Shammi.

A wisp of a smile played on Nimmo's face as she finished braiding a parandi into her hair. Her mother stood in the doorway holding a bowl of freshly-cooked karah parshad covered with a muslin cloth. Inhaling the delicious aroma of the parshad, Nimmo rose hurriedly and adjusted her veil over her head to join her mother.

"Come, let's go to the gurudwara before it gets too hot," said Chinti. "A lakh of thanks to Waheguru for finding such a good match for you. I must keep my promise to offer karah parshad and rumala at the gurudwara."

"Thank Waheguru at least one burden will be off our backs," added Maji.

Trying to hide the excitement bubbling in her heart, Nimmo along with her sister Bholan followed Chinti to the village gurudwara. The Zaildarni was a major donor and commanded a privileged position in the Gurudwara.

The Gurudwara was a brick building with a large central dome on its roof, flanked by four smaller ones on the corners. A deep verandah running on three sides came in useful to serve langar. There was a large congregation hall with the Guru Granth Sahib placed at one end and a small two-room quarter at the back for the granthi. The Nishan Sahib, mounted with a Khanda, stood tall in the large walled courtyard which had several sheesham trees and a small well in the corner. A huge pipal spread its branches wide over a brick platform around its massive trunk.

The gurudwara was the centre of major religious, social and cultural activity in the village. Men lounged around after paying obeisance, discussing the falling moral standards of youngsters and unholy rampage of Kalyug. Daring protests by the freedom fighters and heavy-handed suppression by the British government was discussed in hushed tones. The older ones doubted that the gora sarkar could ever be driven out, while the younger lot claimed that India would stop at nothing less than complete freedom. Children came here for elementary studies, and the panchayat held meetings to decide collective village issues and settle petty personal feuds, mostly on land encroachments and division of canal water.

Bhai ji, as all courteously addressed the granthi, was a middle-aged, sagacious looking man with a long, white beard, dressed in a white kurta-pyjama, blue turban and a kirpan slung across his shoulder. He always had a kind word for all. He blessed Nimmo and Bholan and doled out some patasa parshad for them.

Suddenly they heard a commotion outside with loud voices and screams. They rushed out to see a group of people dragging and thrashing Bhinda in front of the Gurudwara gate. Bhinda belonged to the chamar community who skinned dead animals and disposed of their carcasses. He was trying to hold off the blows and begging to be heard.

"Stop, good men, calm down and tell me what the matter is," asked Bhai ji. "It is not correct to resort to violence in front of the House of God. What wrong has he done?"

"Bhai ji, today early morning as I was going to my fields, I saw someone with his face covered slink out of the Gurudwara," said Major Singh. "I stopped to see who it was so early in the morning. He ran when he saw me, but I followed him and recognized him. I waited to get some other people together and bring him to you. This son-of-a-bitch chamar has defiled our Gurudwara by setting his dirty feet in it. We should skin him alive for his audacity!" Many others joined in the clamour.

"Hanji, we will break his bones. How did this bastard have the courage to enter this holy place? He must be taught a lesson that his coming generations will remember."

"Listen to me, good men," said Bhai ji. "You all come and listen to the Guru's bani here in this Gurudwara, but you have failed to follow its message. Gurbani tells you that there is no difference between men; all are equal in God's house. Let him go."

"But why did you come here early in the morning even before the Gurudwara opened? Did you come to steal?" asked Chinti.

"No, Zaildarni ji, I swear by Waheguru, may my hands fall off, and worms run in my body if I lie, I did not come to steal."

"Then, why did you come? You know you should not enter the Gurudwara."

"My little boy is very ill since last week," said Bhinda. "Last night his fever shot up alarmingly. We tried to bathe his forehead with a wet cloth and gave him the Hakim's medicine, but nothing worked. My wife has much faith in the Guru. She pleaded with me to go pray for his health at the Gurudwara and bring some dust from the doorstep. I could not say no to a distraught mother and came to beg the Guru to cure my son."

Everyone was quiet for a moment, at a loss for what to say. Nimmo felt very sad for the man. How could some people lay greater claim to God than others? If he created all living beings, surely he belonged to all of them equally? What was the use of reading or listening to Gurbani every day if people did not believe and follow it?

"Go back to your houses and leave the man alone," said Bhai ji. "Bhinde, wait here till I fetch some parshad for your son. I shall pray for his health."

2

Sojourn to a City

Zaildar Kehar Singh and Mian Ali Beg were both members of the Unionist Party and often sat together to discuss politics over a couple of drinks. Both held progressive, secular views and opposed the two-nation theory raised by the All India Muslim League. How could anyone separate a people who lived together like brothers for centuries? Was it possible to tear away nails from flesh? Women from both Zaildar's and Ali Beg's house often sat together to embroider and weave after finishing their household chores. Mithai and karah parshad was sent to Mian's family on occasions like Sangrand and Diwali, and Sakina's ammi Hajjo would send fruit and uncooked food to Chinti on Eid. They accepted it without the rancour that Hindus and Sikhs would not eat food cooked in a Muslim kitchen where beef and halal meat was cooked. The Hindu-Sikh traditions being more prevalent, few Muslim women wore a burkha in the village. However, some from highly-placed families opted for a chadar over their regular salwar suit and dupatta.

Nimmo loved the vermicelli Hajjo massi cooked at Eid, and promptly arrived to claim her share.

"Nee, your Maji may get angry if she finds out you are eating in our home," said Sakina's ammi lightly as she handed her a large bowl of vermicelli cooked in milk, almonds and sultanas.

Nimmo shrugged off her warnings with a giggle and reached eagerly for the bowl.

"Who will tell her, massi?"

"Take this dry fruit for your Bebe when you go back," said Hajjo, handing her a bowl.

Sakina had a younger sister, Shammi, and two older brothers. Children from both families had grown up playing together. Akhtar and Waseem often sat around in the outer courtyard where the girls played stapu and geete. Akhtar was a young, college-going boy of eighteen, sharp-featured and well-built with an athletic body. He was friendly and outgoing, easily winning people's hearts with his social courtesies and helpful nature. A hero to his sisters and younger brother Waseem, Akhtar had made a special place in Nimmo's heart too. All of them listened spellbound when he narrated the valour of the Gadhari Babbe and Neta ji Subhash Chander Bose's Indian National Army in the struggle for independence.

As Nimmo stepped into adolescence, she became conscious and careful about her dress and appearance when going to Sakina's house. She often caught Akhtar looking at her longer than a casual glance, and her heart fluttered with a new felt excitement. Chinti was too busy with her unending chores to police the girls and didn't seem to realize that they had turned into young women. The eagle-eyed Maji, however, did not fail to monitor their moves.

"Nee Chinti, are you blind? Can you not see that the girls have grown as tall as the roof and still run around in the village like unbridled mares? When are you going to teach them some modesty? I shall break their ankles if I see them stepping into Mian's house after today. Don't you realize they have two young boys?"

"Must you make such a big issue out of nothing, Maji?" replied Chinti churlishly. "The girls have been playing in each other's homes since they were as high as my knee. You don't like the sight of them, that's all."

Nimmo and Bholan's visits to Sakina's home became less frequent, depending on when they could sneak out without Maji finding out. Nimmo missed these visits for more than just Sakina's company and the vermicelli. She missed seeing Akhtar, his stolen glances and lighthearted teasing, and often found reasons to go up to the roof in the hope that she would catch sight of him. When she did, she would blush and turn back as soon as he looked towards her. By and by, both of them tuned their roof visits to late afternoons, when the families rested indoors. Each afternoon at a defined hour after lunch, they would climb up and look out for each other, smiling and standing around for some time, mindless of the sharp afternoon sun and scorching heat. There was no dialogue, no letters exchanged. Sometimes they would playfully throw small pebbles at each other. Nimmo had been secretly embroidering a handkerchief for Akhtar which she carefully wrapped around a pebble and threw across to him. Akhtar caught it expertly and broke out in a delighted smile when he untied the handkerchief. He held it to his heart and then kissed it. Nimmo smiled, blushed and ran down the stairs. Both were aware of the vast religious and communal chasm between their families and knew that they would not fathom it in a hundred years. But an ephemeral, unde-fined thread connected their hearts, bringing excitement and some succour to the desperate and hopeless longings of early youth.

There were not many opportunities for Nimmo to step across the limits of her small village, except for rare occasions when she accompanied her mother to her grand-parent's village or attended weddings in neighbouring vil-lages or cities. So Nimmo and Bholan were delighted when Chinti agreed to take them along on a trip to Ludhiana.

Two handsome white bullocks were saddled to a rath and controlled by the rathwan with a whip. The wooden rath was decorated with brass inlay work and had a domed roof covered with decorative cloth trimmed with cowl shells. Chinti, Nimmo and Bholan settled on a mattress spread out inside, peeping out of the small, curtained win-dows as the wooden wheels rattled across the narrow, brick-paved lanes.

Once out of the village boundary, they moved on to a mud path that wound through many fields and villages be-fore finally connecting with the main Grand Trunk road. The track was replete with potholes and deep ruts formed by wheels of endless passing bullock carts, creating puddles of muddy water during monsoons. Rows of dark and hardy kikar, tall sheesham and majestic pipal trees lined the long dirt path, their leaves rustling in the hot summer breeze. They crossed a massive, gnarled pipal tree with a brick platform around it and a water pump close by for weary travellers to stop for a breather and a drink of water before continuing with their journey. Digging a well or having a water pump installed for the public was believed to be an act of great charity, and this one had a slab of stone inscribed with "Installed by Sardar Karam Singh in memory of his late father Sardar Sardul Singh of village Raipur".

The horizon stretched till as far as the eye could see. Verdant fields of wheat and fodder stretched far, alternating with gently rolling sand dunes and open grassy patches where herds of buffaloes grazed peacefully. An occasional farmer could be seen ploughing a field with bullocks yoked to a wooden plough, twisting their tails and making a clucking noise to urge them to move faster. Chamar women sat on their haunches in the open spaces, using their sickles to cut grass for their cattle. They worked in groups of three or four, with their 'chadar' knotted around their heads to form a type of pouch behind their backs, in which they kept tossing bunches of grass. Nimmo and Chinti peeped out curiously at the occasional tonga, bullock cart, horse rider or cyclist they crossed on the way. Foot travellers carrying cloth bundles on their heads looked up at the lucky passengers of the rath with curious and wistful eyes.

The rath finally rolled on to the Grand Trunk road, built on an embankment to escape the danger of floods. Nimmo gaped wide-eyed at the buses, trucks and lorries whizzing past them. They slowly reached the city roads where tonga-wallahs hurled obscenities at their emaciated horses urging them to move faster, and axles of cotton laden carts groaned and creaked, splashing muddy puddle water onto angry pedestrians.

Ludhiana, named after the Lodhi Dynasty who founded the city in 1480, was bedazzling with its glamour of billboards and swanky shops in the Chaura Bazaar. The tall, majestic Clock Tower beautifully made in red brick-work with a huge clock on the top stood as an iconic land-mark of the city. The roads were alive and bustling with shoppers and hawkers selling their wares on the roadside. Nimmo pointed towards some smartly dressed women riding in cycle rickshaws:

"Look Bebe, they do not even cover their heads with a dupatta!"

Bholan could not stop gaping at the huge film posters on the roadside showing the ravishingly beautiful and pop-ular heroine Noorjehan.

"Hai, behen, just see how beautiful she is!"

Once in a while, a government vehicle would drive up to their village and set up a screen to show some old Hindi movies, and small documentaries on social issues like health, education and government projects. These movies were awaited with much excitement, and the women would hurriedly wind up their evening chores so as not to miss out on any part.

The girls begged Chinti to stop for lemon soda bottles with a marble on top, and the rathwan drew up the rath on the roadside. As they stepped down, they started hearing loud slogans from the Chaura Bazaar side. Soon a proces-sion of khadi-clad men and women emerged, carrying placards and shouting slogans for the British to quit India.

"Gore hakam Bharat chchor!"

"Bharat Mata ki jai!"

"Gandhi ji ki jai!"

"Todi bachcha hai hai!"

"Bebe who are these people?" asked Bholan.

"They are followers of Gandhi and want to drive out the angrez from the country," replied Chinti. "The rani in vilayat is very powerful and I doubt the gori sarkar can ever be driven out."

The atmosphere seemed electrified with nationalistic fervour as people rushed out of their shops and houses to watch the satyagrahis. The demonstration swelled as more people joined them. The anger and enthusiasm were infectious, and many onlookers joined in raising slogans. Suddenly people saw a curl of smoke go up from the direction of the Railway Station, and there were shouts of "Fire! Fire!" The fire brigade soon arrived with a screeching fire alarm and mounted police rode in, using a water cannon to disperse the demonstrators. Gunshots sounded in the distance resulting in complete pandemonium. As the crowd panicked, there was angry shouting and screaming, and people started to run helter-skelter, leaving the main road to disappear into the narrow bylanes. Many fell in the stampede, and there were cries for help as others ran over them—the sound of breaking glass and neighing of horses added to the din. Shopkeepers quickly retreated into their shops and downed their shutters. Stunned and confused by the complete mayhem, the rathwan waited to find a safe way out from this chaos and Nimmo, Chinti and Bholan sat terrified in the rath, peeping out from behind the curtains. The girls clung to Chinti, their hearts hammering in their chests.

After the crowd had dispersed and the police had galloped away further down the road, Nimmo saw a satyagrahi lying by the roadside. He seemed to be injured and was groaning.

"Bebe, let's help get him away from here to some doctor," said Nimmo.

"No, no, girl let him be. Let's not ask for trouble. The police has not gone far yet."

"How can we leave him here, Bebe? We must help." Despite her fear, she felt enraged and fired by nationalistic fervour. Jumping down from the rath without waiting for an answer, Nimmo called out to the rathwan to help the man. Putting him in the rath, they drove away from the main road towards the Do Moria Pul.

The young man was dark-skinned with a short, thin frame, dressed in a khadi kurta-pyjama and wearing a khadi cap. No one would have given him a second look in a gathering.

"Who are you, son? Are you hurt?" Chinti asked the stranger.

"I am one of the many Indian slaves fighting for freedom from the British Empire," he replied. "I have sustained more injuries to my respect and honour than my body. These firangis have looted and defiled our country for centuries, and I have sworn to stake my life to push them out and reclaim our sovereignty."

"What is your religion, son?"

"My religion and identity is Hindustani; nothing else. Please join the struggle for liberating our country."

Nimmo listened to him spellbound.

"Where can we drop you?"

"Please drop me right here. I am very grateful to you for your help."

Nimmo looked at him admiringly as he thanked them and limped away into a side street.

"Seems to be a chamar from his looks and style of speaking," said Chinti.

"But much more courageous than Jat landowners who have sold their self-respect to the British for jagirs," replied Nimmo.

"Hear this girl speak! What do you understand about these affairs? It's not so easy to drive away the angrez. These young men are just risking their lives and creating unnecessary trouble for everyone."

3

Nimmo's Engagement

In the nearby village of Raipur, Sardar Naib Singh's son Hukum Singh had been newly commissioned into the army as a Second Lieutenant. Naib Singh and his wife Jeeti were looking for a suitable bride for him. The nai had been briefed that it was of prime importance that the girl should be of 'good bone'; meaning thereby, of good genetic stock. That would include a review of genealogical data going back two generations, land holdings, reputation and social standing of the family. They had mulled over many matches suggested by the nai and shortlisted Zaildar Kehar Singh's daughter Nimmo as a potential bride for their son.

The Zaildar's family met the benchmarks of good social status, large land holdings and a healthy hereditary line. Not wanting to rely on the nai's panegyrics alone, Naib Singh asked his wife and sister to go and check out the girl. There was no tradition of the boy and girl meeting with each other before marriage, the word of the match-maker often being enough. This, of course, was a special case due to the high rank of the boy in question, warrant-ing a visit by his mother and aunt to see the girl. The nai was sent to fix a date for a visit. Bebe Jeeti and her widowed sister-in-law, who lived with them and was known as 'Bhua' by the whole village, donned their voluminous gha-gras and embroidered chadars to go to Sahnewal. The family rath, with an embellished canopy and driven by a pair of handsome bullocks, was summoned to ferry them to the Zaildar's haveli. A nain accompanied Jeeti and Bhua, as it was customary for ladies from the Jat landlord families to be accompanied by their nains on their sojourns to attend weddings, deaths and births, as maids-in-wait-ing.

"My malik has found a girl like a lachchmi for your son, Sardarni ji," said the nain. "You cannot find such a girl if you search for her with a lighted lamp! She is tall and slim like the sarooh tree and submissive as a cow. And what a well-to-do and high family she belongs to! They are known in fifty villages around. The Zaildar owns a jagir and more than thirty cattle—they will fill your house with dowry. The whole village will remember this wedding."

"I believe you, Rani," replied Jeeti. "But I do hope Hukum likes her. You know fauj has made him think like a sahib, and he has to socialize with highly-placed officers. The girl is not much educated."

"What will a girl do with too much education except get out of hand? This girl is much better than spoilt city girls who don't know how to respect their elders, Sardarni ji. You should be careful not to let your son fall into their trap. And let me tell you I want a pair of gold earrings for this wedding."

The nai and nain were undisputed masters-of-ceremonies in the village. In a stratified society with designated roles for all, the nai and nain, even though they came from a lower caste, held a position of much importance. They were referred to as raja rani and handsomely rewarded with gifts and money at social ceremonies. The nais were dispatched to various out-of-village relatives and friends with both good and bad news, and were, in the process, well-travelled and socially connected. The nains were experts in intricately braiding women's hair, sometimes with a saggi-phul pinioned on top of the head for brides. Girls were mostly married young, and the nain accompanied them to their in-laws after the wedding, helping them with their grooming. A harbinger of all marriages, deaths, births and religious ceremonies in the village, the nain could be often seen swaying through the lanes balancing a large wicker basket of laddoos on her head. She would step through the door of a village house and announce her arrival in a high octave.

"I bow to your feet, Bibi. The sardars of the outer high haveli have had a grandson. His Chchati is to be held two days from today. There is an invitation for all of you to attend." She would then proceed to set down her basket, hand out their share of six or twelve laddoos, share the latest village news, gather updates on the family bulletin and move on to the next house.

Jeeti and Bhua reached the Zaildar's haveli well before noon. After a vigorous hugging ritual one shoulder to the other, they were respectfully ushered into the baithak and served sherbet and several homemade snacks. They looked around the house unabashedly, assessing the number of rooms and evaluating the furniture. It was a large haveli with a huge courtyard and arched verandas. The baithak was set with upholstered wooden sofas and chairs, with an imported chandelier hanging from the roof. A large painting of Guru Nanak Dev was placed prominently on the mantelpiece, flanked by a pair of finely etched Moradabadi brass tumblers. They proceeded to ask about the details and welfare of the family. Maji and Chinti made similar enquiries about their family in return. Several links of distant common relatives were found and exclaimed upon. Within the first half-hour of conversation, the women had discovered that the two families shared six different relatives. In some time Nimmo was ushered in, clad in a printed cheent shirt and black soof salwar, her head coyly covered with a net dupatta edged with crochet lace. The trend of wearing matching salwar-kameez suits was not the norm yet, coming in later from the royal city of Patiala. Unmarried girls wore no makeup, and any attempt at dolling up was frowned upon.

Chinti proudly recounted Nimmo's literary achievements as she piled some more savouries into Jeeti's plate.

"She can read the Gurbani fluently, read and write Punjabi and also add and subtract. We do not believe in keeping our daughters uneducated like dumb cattle ji."

"I have been suffering from knee pain for the last two years and handed over most of the kitchen duties to her," added Chinti.

Nimmo's other essential qualifications for making a

good daughter-in-law were elucidated upon with tangible proof. A pair of doves made in stuffed satin and embellished with beadwork sat beak-to-beak in a picture hanging proudly over the main door.

The mantelpiece, covered with a thick white cotton cloth embroidered with floral patterns and crocheted lace edging, provided a display platform for various artefacts. There was no household craft the girl did not know, the khes spread on the bed having been woven by her talented hands too. Bholan, eavesdropping on their conversation from behind the door, stifled her giggles on hearing that all crafts work done by other females of the house was Nimmo's.

Suitably impressed with the majestic haveli, the furnishings and the maids in attendance, Jeeti sized up the girl, tall and slim like a young tree in first bloom. Her body was well-proportioned and filled out in the right places. She had sharply defined features with a high forehead and cheekbones. The eyes, though not too large, were a warm cinnamon colour, with arched eyebrows and a doe-like innocence to them.

Jeeti wavered a while. Her family was acknowledged for their fair complexion, earning the nickname *bagge* in the village. This girl's skin was the colour of tea with too little milk. Would her son like her? But then, who wanted a daughter-in-law to rule her son's heart through beauty and wiles? It was enough for the girl to be strong and healthy to bear strong sons. Moreover, Sardar ji's massi was already pressurizing them to accept her niece, but Jeeti did not want any girl from her in-law's family to set foot in her house. Her late mother-in-law, who had brought her much grief, had belonged to the Grewal clan, known for their intriguing and devious minds. Fearing that Sardar ji would succumb to his massi's manipulations, she felt it necessary to clinch the match before things went out of her hands. Besides, one did not go by the girl alone; the family background was most important when making a marriage relationship, and families of status and good repute were hard to find. She could not help but note that the Zaildar had no son, and his daughters would benefit from his vast landholdings. She made up her mind.

"Come and sit next to me, Biba. You are our daughter now." She rose to caress Nimmo's head and placed a silver coin in her hand. "May your husband and brother live forever."

"The girl is a virtual Lachchmi. God bless you. May you bring good luck and prosperity to your home and hearth," exclaimed Bhua, taking the cue and rising to hug Nimmo.

"May Waheguru make this match lucky for both families, Sardarni ji," said the nain, taking the plate of laddoos around for everyone to sweeten their mouths on the auspicious occasion. "Lakhs of congratulations to both the families. Matches are all preordained by destiny."

Bholan and the cleaning woman Jamalo, who had been lurking behind the door, rushed in to congratulate everyone.

"Allah bless you sardarni ji, many congratulations. May both your families prosper and grow!" said Jamalo, hoping for a baksheesh.

There was more hugging with renewed gusto. Jeeti gave a silver rupee to Jamalo, who responded with a string

of blessings. Thus Nimmo, all of sixteen years, was be-
trothed to Lt. Hukum Singh of Raipur.

Hukum Singh was the first boy from his village to
graduate from the Government College, Ludhiana. His recruitment into the Army as a commissioned officer was a
matter of much pride for the family.

The Indian Army originated in the Indian rebellion of
1857, often called the Indian Mutiny in British history.
The Crown took over direct rule of British India from the
East India Company in 1858. Before that, the Company
controlled and operated precursor units of the Indian
Army alongside units of the British Army. The uprisings
of 1857 led the British to discontinue recruitments from
Awadh, Bihar, Central and South India which they declared to be non-martial races, while Sikhs, Gurkhas and
Pathans were declared martial races and given preference
for recruitment. All three races were recognized and rewarded for their help in quelling the rebellion. The Khalsa
army had nearly defeated the British during the two Anglo-Sikh wars in the 1840s. With over 2000 British soldiers killed in the battle of Ferozshah in the First Anglo-
Sikh war and over 3000 in the battle of Chillianwallah in
the second Anglo-Sikh war, these encounters brought
about begrudging respect in the Britishers for the Sikh soldier. The discipline, training and hardiness of the Sikh
Army impressed them a lot, and they were seen as a reassuring alternative after the mass rebellion of the Bengal
army and the uprising of the central provinces.

Up until the Second World War, Indians were recruited up to the rank of JCO. The dire need for military
personnel during the war forced the British to offer several

allurements to Indians, including the promise of complete independence. Young men from well-to-do families with proven loyalties to the British were commissioned as officers in the British-Indian Army. The Britishers were particular to recruit officers from desirable backgrounds, promoting elitism. Army jobs were much sought after by Jat Sikhs, who perceived themselves as a martial race upholding the spirit of bravery and sacrifice bestowed by Guru Gobind Singh upon the 'Khalsa.' The rural Punjabi male made a good fit for the army being physically strong, well-built and bold, and a soldier's persona enhanced his macho image. In need of soldiers for the war, the Britishers motivated them to join the army by bestowing jagirs or land endowments on them for loyalty and valour in battle—a great inducement for the land-loving Jats.

Educated, professional Jat boys were not easy to come by, and Nimmo's family could hardly believe their luck in finding an army officer for her. In the Jat community, the yardstick for a compatible match was parity between the landholdings of both families, all else came later. Sardar Naib Singh's land holdings were not exactly at par with the Zaildar's, but the boy's job compensated for that. Happy with the nai's report, Nimmo's parents did not feel the necessity to go and see him personally. As per the nai and Nimmo's bhua's brother-in-law, whose wife was from Raipur, Hukum Singh was a tall, fair and handsome man. Whoever did go looking at men's faces? It was a girl's good fortune if the man was good-looking, but it was certainly not something that would affect his matrimonial prospects. Hukum Singh was ten years older to her, but that was not a major concern. A popular Punjabi saying was that 'Men and horses never grow old.' Caste, family background, land holdings, job and status, these were all that mattered.

Nimmo was giddy with excitement. What glamour, what presence the faujis had in their starched green uniforms, brass epaulettes and shining brown leather boots which went tak-tak when they walked! Her aunt's daughter was married to a fauji, and she had heard her tell fascinating stories about faraway places which she had travelled with him. She occasionally visited the village dressed in smart suits, carrying a fancy purse and wearing ballerinas. Her husband looked dashing in a neatly tied turban, and they rode in a tonga from the railway station rather than walk like most of the village folk. Girls had a great fascination for Army men, and they were heroes of many songs and bolis.

Chunj teri ve kaleya kaavan
Sone naal marahwan,
Ja aakheen mere dhol sipahi nu,
Maen nit aussiyan paavan
Ohdi khabar liyade kaavan
Tenu gheo di churi paavan

(O black crow.
I will cover your beak in gold
If you carry a message to my soldier
And tell him I wait for him each day.
If you bring me news about him,
I will feed you with butter and sweet bread.)

4

Wedding Vows

Nimmo's wedding was scheduled to be held soon after the Rabi harvest brought in the cash. Her family went into a frenzy of preparations. Aunts, sisters-in-law and cousins were summoned to help and prepare her trousseau dresses. Her mother, wise to the needs of two marriageable daughters, had already prepared twenty-one bedding sets and hundred-and-one kitchen utensils. A generous number of beddings and utensils were a major part of any Jat girl's trousseau, as hosting house guests was routine, and it was a huge embarrassment to run short of decent bedding for them. Women spent long hours weaving khes and daris and embroidering bed sheets for their trousseau. The village carpenter made a brass knobbed charkha and two large, painted wooden boxes for the bridal trousseau. Nimmo was threading the last stitches into an exquisite phulkari. In contrast to the other bright colours, she made this bit in black to ward off the evil eye. Amazingly, the pattern was not traced on the cloth, and women created perfectly shaped geometrical designs by counting threads as they embroidered. Phulkaris were worn with great pride by women in all of Punjab right up to Afghanistan.

"Biba ji, you are going to be our guest only for a few more days now. This house will be very forlorn. Sakina will be lonely without you. Yesterday when I went to work at their house, Akhtar was also asking about you. He said he hadn't seen you around for many days now," said Jamalo with a hint of slyness.

Nimmo's face coloured with embarrassment and she hurriedly got up to fetch some leftover rotis and lentils for her. She did not wish to be reminded of what had to be left behind as part of her childhood.

The Zaildar was leaving for Ludhiana to buy some gold jewellery for Nimmo. It was not the tradition for women to go to the market to choose their clothes or jewellery, which were generally bought by men. They only bought cheaper stuff from the village vendors. The more expensive fabric was imported from England or Japan and available in city markets. Indian high-end woven fabric like Kimkhwab and Benarasi silk came from Benaras, and only the elite afforded them. Women stitched the dresses themselves, or, for expensive marriage clothing, hired the village tailor of the Cheemba caste..

"Ask her if she wants anything special for her jewellery," he asked Chinti, shy of asking Nimmo directly about her trousseau.

Nimmo, who was standing close by, turned to him excitedly. "Bapu ji, I want pipal patti jhumkas!"

Maji, hobbling across the yard with her walking stick, stopped to admonish her.

"Look at this shameless girl clamouring for jewellery! This is what kalyug is all about. Girls have no shame about opening their mouths and speaking about their weddings! We will soon have them picking their grooms too! When we were young, we would never dare to make any demand, much less speak about our wedding jewellery. Sit back quietly. Your father will get what he has to. You remember I attended my sister's grandson's marriage in the baar last year? Girls were so bashful there that the bride wore a burkha for her lawan. "

Chinti knew better than to confront her mother-in-law and hastened to chastise Nimmo.

"Now that you are going to another house, you had better learn to keep a check on your tongue, girl."

"But what is the baar, Maji?" asked Nimmo, refusing to be quietened.

"The fertile regions developed by canal irrigation including Sargodha, Faislabad, Nankana Sahib, Pak Pattan, Toba Tek Singh and many more are the baar," said Maji. "The villages there are called chak and given numbers. The angrez honoured my sister's father-in-law with fifty acres of good land in Chak 28 after he retired from the army. He had fought in Waziristan and taken four bullet wounds. Kehar son, I hope you are taking someone with you to the town. You can't be too careful with the threat of dacoits looming large. Do make sure to get back before sunset."

"Don't worry, Maji. When will I get a chance to use my double-bore gun? And who can match the speed of my mare in a radius of ten villages around here?" laughed the

Zaildar.

Nama Chacha, who had been sitting quietly in a corner, suddenly picked up a stick and rushed towards the Zaildar.

"Tha! Tha! Tha! Let the dacoits shoot you dead! Shoot you dead forever! I hope you never come back," he cried, holding out the stick like a gun.

The Zaildar snatched the stick from his hands and hit him repeatedly till he fell to the ground, crying out beseechingly,

"Stop, please stop. I will be quiet!"

Maji rushed to hold back the Zaildar, "Don't hit him Kesar! Will you kill him now? He is your younger brother. You know he doesn't know what he is saying."

"Why did you allow him to step out of his room?" shouted the Zaildar. "You know I can't stand him. Get him out of my sight."

Nama was snivelling and had wet his pyjamas in fear. Maji helped him up and took him to his room.

Bholan and her cousin left their game of geete and disappeared inside the house in fear. Every one waited for the Zaildar to leave before resuming with whatever they were doing. Chinti ignored the incident and continued to oil Nimmo's hair and check for lice. Maji pulled up a peehri close to her spinning wheel and started drawing out long cotton threads which she kept winding around a spool.

"I don't know what demons posses Kehar when he sees Nama," said Maji. "The poor man is terrified of him. Why lose temper with someone who is not in control of his senses? I have asked him so many times to take him to the hospital in Ludhiana for treatment. His ailment is not something the village hakim can understand."

"Bapu should not beat up Chacha so mercilessly, Bebe. I get so terrified when he turns wild like this. Why does he hate him so?" asked Nimmo.

"It's none of your business. Keep out of elders' affairs," said Chinti.

"Ouch Bebe! You are pulling my hair!" cried Nimmo.

"You had better grow up now, girl. Learn to be resilient. You are going to have to take lots of responsibilities. Don't make a fuss over little things. No one there is going to pamper your attitude."

"Hey sister, I have heard that our brother-in-law can't see from his left eye?" teased Bholan returning to the scene now that her father was gone.

"May your tongue burn, girl," retorted Chinti. "You think the angrez recruit one-eyed boys into their fauj? They check them out like a new silver coin. It is not easy to land a job of a— what do you say, laften!"

Nimmo's aunt paused stitching the gota on a dupatta to voice her own warning.

"They say the big rani in vilayat has given orders for the most handsome young men to be picked and sent to her. She keeps them for as long as she pleases and then gives them to other mems. The mems use black magic to make men forget all about their families back home and entrap them by feeding them chicken and liquor every day. Many times they become so enamoured of the white-skinned mems that they don't return to India at all. Be careful that your husband never crosses the black waters!"

Nimmo was alarmed, but could not react to any remark about her to-be-husband and risk being called a shameless hussy. She blushed and looked the other way whenever anyone mentioned Hukum Singh, though her heartbeat quickened at the mention of his name. She often hung around listening to bits of conversation about him trying to put together an image of the man who would be her husband. Her excitement was tinged with trepidation and a sense of nervousness; would she come up to her college-educated, officer husband's expectations? How would she interact with city people from his circle? Would she be able to uphold the family's honour? Of late, she had often been pulled up by Maji for omissions she had paid no attention to.

"Look at the way she takes huge strides like a camel. Girl, learn to walk gracefully. And don't let the veil slip from your head. You will have many men folk at your in-laws home."

"Hai rabba! Hear that raucous laughter! Keep your voice down, girl. Don't let it reach the men folk in the house. What will your mother-in-law say? Of course, it all depends on what a mother teaches her daughter," Maji added with an accusing look towards her daughter-in-law Chinti.

"Now listen to me carefully. Behave respectfully with all your in-laws. They should not hear a loud voice or a no to anything; 'haanji' is the only word which sounds sweet on a girl's tongue. Be humble and obedient and never, ever show a temper. Realize that a wife's place is at her husband's feet. He is your malik. Keep him happy and deny him nothing. Take good care of his food and clothing. Keep his bedsheets clean, wash your feet at night and be careful not to fart in his bed."

"But what to do if one needs to fart, Maji?" giggled Bholan.

"Just remove yourself from there, foolish girl. Who likes stinky women? Don't give him a reason to beat you. For men it's as easy to change a woman as changing their jutti. Remember, you are responsible for upholding the honour of your father's turban."

"It all depends on a girl's destiny, Maji," said Chinti. "Elders have said that girls with good kismet have ruled, whereas beauties have wept. May Waheguru's grace be on her."

Colourful tents were erected in the backyard, and the cooks built large clay ovens, placing massive iron pots and skillets on the fire for frying various sweetmeats. Curls of smoke from burning dry cotton bush reeds and cow dung patties in clay ovens arose high into the summer sky and announced the beginning of wedding celebrations to the village. A delicious aroma from mounds of fried mithai pervaded the house. Meals were cooked for guests who had arrived weeks earlier to help with the wedding preparations. It was a tradition to gift all relatives at least five seers of dry sweet and salted savouries, which were prepared weeks in advance.

Sakina, Shammi, Tippi and Baggi all came over to see Nimmo's trousseau. They were fascinated to see the bridal salwar kameez in deep red Kimkhwab, a deep blue ghagra with a broad gota border and a parrot green velvet shirt with zardozi embroidery around the neck. Nimmo excitedly showed off her suits in the popular fabrics of the day, like Dhoop Chaaon, Teri Meri Marzi, Dil ki Pyaas and Aankh ka Nasha. Brides were not generally measured for their trousseau clothing, which was stitched to a loose, standard size so that the expensive suits continued to fit through the post-wedding addition to the girth. The girls touched and marvelled at her gold ornaments. There were the 'Chaunk' and 'Phul', which included a central dome-shaped head adornment with two smaller ones worn on the side, all attached by black strings to the hair braid to keep them securely in place. There was also a stunning 'Guluband' (choker necklace), and 'Nant' (armlets), 'Bankan' (heavy bracelets), a 'Tadaghi' (waist girdle) and 'Lachhe' (anklets). Not familiar with any cosmetics, the girls were curious about trying out the popular facial cream 'Afghan Snow' which was part of Nimmo's makeup. They dipped their fingers in it, rubbed it on their faces and giggled at themselves in the mirror. Use of cosmetics was the prerogative of married women, who used it with much discretion so as not to appear audacious. Sakina tried out a pair of Khussa, a Punjabi Jutti embroidered in gold and red, with an upturned toe.

Nimmo's days were a haze of excitement with her new clothes, jewellery and dreams of her future husband. The surreptitious trips to the roof stood abandoned, and Akhtar had fast faded out of her mind. A young heart can experience flitting emotions, easily carried away from one to another, being equally passionate about both at a given time. Nimmo was riding a wave of delicious anticipation of an exciting future with her husband. One afternoon when she was sitting alone, Jamalo put down her broom after sweeping the courtyard and came and squatted near her.

"Akhtar was asking if you could meet him once," she

whispered. "My heart goes out to him. But it is all Allah's will. Be happy in your new life."

Annoyed and embarrassed by her persistent audacity, Nimmo ignored her. A fortnight before the wedding, Nimmo was rubbed with chickpea and turmeric paste each evening by women relatives and friends. This tradition of applying vatna, was supposed to lighten up and brighten the bride's complexion. Women gathered to dance the giddha, venting suppressed feelings through bawdy songs and cheeky bolis romancing their lovers, damning their mothers-in-law and taking obscene digs at brothers-in-laws. Nimmo felt a thrill pass through her body when the girls sang a song about her lover renouncing the world for her:

Sunh heeray, teri preet da mareya
ni ranjha jogi hoyeya,
Sawa ranjha jogi hoyeya ...
Sunh heeray, teri preet da mareya

Nimmo tried to put up a show of grief for leaving her parental home, but all that she felt was an eagerness to break free of the constraints and monotony of village life and step into a new world with her husband. Sixteen years was a long enough time to spend trailing her mother doing household chores! She was bursting with curiosity about the city of Ambala where she would eventually go after her marriage to Hukum Singh, who was posted in the cantonment there. So far, her interaction with boys had been limited to formal pleasantries with her cousins and flirtation with Akhtar. She daydreamed about Hukum Singh; what would it be like to be held by him? Thinking of him made her heart beat faster. Did he drink a lot? Would he beat her if she made a mistake? It was okay for a man to hit his wife in anger occasionally, but she prayed that he would not be too foul-tempered. Anyway, she was determined to do all she could to please him.

The previous monsoon, her father's younger sister Nikki bhua had arrived unannounced one day with bruises on her face, wailing about having been thrashed by her husband and vowing never to set foot in his house again. Maji had let off a string of abuses for her son-in-law, but did not counter the Zaildar when he said:

"Quarrels between couples are a normal affair. So what if he hit you a little? He is your malik after all, and you are not dead, are you? Try not to anger him and learn to be humble and tolerant. It is a shame for a woman to walk out of her home for such trivial reasons. We have two daughters to marry off yet. What example are you setting for them? If you don't want to be hit, control your tongue and obey him."

After a week of cajoling and counselling, Nikki bhua was sent back to her husband with a tin of ghee and some sweets made by the village halwai.

Nimmo's wedding regaled the village with much feasting and merry-making. She was up early on the day of her wedding and cleaned her teeth with a neem twig. The nain was there to wash her hair with sour curds and give a vigorous scrub to her body. Her long black hair was dried by sitting her near an angeethi and oiled to a shine. The nain parted them in the middle, made several fine braids on either side, and secured a gold saggi phul on the centre of her head by weaving its strings in fine side-braids. These were then knotted into a back braid with a parandi. This hair-style was so securely in place that she would not need to redo it for another fortnight. Her eyes were lined with kohl, and her mami put on red and ivory choora bangles on her slim wrists. Long golden cap-shaped kaleere and dried coconuts were tied to her bangles with red mauli for luck. They swung with a tinkling sound when she walked.

Chinti gasped when she saw her daughter step out in her red bridal salwar suit, a dupatta in gota-jaal drawn low over her forehead, and a magnificent, elaborate phulkari draped over her shoulders. When had she transformed from an awkward, unkempt girl into this pretty young woman standing at the threshold of a new life? She hastily fetched some smouldering red chillies and swirled them around Nimmo's head to ward off the evil eye.

The bursting of firecrackers in the sky and the re-sounding beat of drums heralded the arrival of Nimmo's baraat. Women climbed onto the roofs to watch the pro-cession, while youngsters, old men and children spilt out on to the lanes. They were mighty impressed by the tall, strapping groom riding a white mare atop a red and gold embroidered saddle cloth. He wore a pink turban with a golden aigrette, a sehra of jasmine flowers strings covering his face. The baraat was preceded by a band with men wearing smart red waistcoats, white fitted trousers and smart turbans with raised golden canopies and long flow-ing ends. A troupe of men carried blazing gas lights to light the way. Two nautch girls dressed in gharara suits and elaborate jewellery danced to a popular film song ahead of the procession.

"Maar katari mar jaana, yeh akhiyan kisi se milaana na,

ho, milaana na...,"

An old man with half his teeth missing tried to push past the crowd to look at the dancers.

"It's the well known Rukhsana kanjari from Kanpur! They say she takes five hundred rupees for one dance!"

"Wah Bapu!" laughed a youngster. "You seem to have known her well in your younger days."

The band was followed by baraatis smartly turned out in pink turbans, bund gala coats and fitted pyjamas. Some older ones wore kurtas over loosely-draped lachas knotted at the waist. Their new leather juttis, embroidered in gold thread and curled up at the toe, made a crunching sound with every step. Occasionally someone would fire a rifle shot into the air as a mark of celebration. Bholan and Sakina had been watching from the roof to get a glimpse of the groom. They ran in excitedly to give an update to Nimmo.

"Hai nee, your groom is as handsome as a prince!" said Sakina. "He sits so regally on the white steed in a pink turban and white achkan. He is holding a red velvet-covered sword and has a canopy over his head. It is such a grand baraat! Your destiny was certainly written with a golden pen!"

There were some drunken brawls and score-settling among the gathered relatives, but these were the norm and not taken seriously by anyone. By the next afternoon, lavaan had been solemnized and the baraat fed. Women sang sad farewell songs, and Chinti hugged Nimmo and blessed her as she was carried by her maternal uncle and placed in the doli. The brass-bell necklaces around the necks of the caparisoned pair of white bullocks tinkled as the rath carried Nimmo on to a new phase in her young life. Villagers followed the doli to the outskirts of the village to see her off. Sardar Naib Singh circled a fistful of coins around the groom's head and threw them behind in the brick-paved lane. The village children raced and jostled each other to grab them as the rath drove out of the village. Akhtar did not attend the wedding. He stood at his window, watching the rath get smaller and smaller till it disappeared from sight. He had not even said goodbye to her.

5

A New Life

The wedding party reached Raipur before sunset. Though many of the baraatis were armed with rifles, a constant threat of dacoits made it dangerous to travel after dark, and wedding parties took care to be back safely before darkness set in. Women welcomed the couple by singing wedding songs in long drawn-out, keening nasal notes. Hukum Singh's mother, Bebe Jeeti, waited at the door covered with a pink dupatta edged with gota lace. She poured mustard oil on both sides of the entrance and circled a tumbler of water around the head of the groom and bride to ward off the evil eye. A bunch of eunuchs made a clamorous show of clapping and danced provocatively to bawdy songs. Mirasis entertained the guests by poking fun at various relatives and singing popular ballads like Sohni Mahiwal and Roop Basant, receiving some grain and food for their efforts.

Wrapped up in her red gota jaal dupatta and salu, Nimmo sat still and demure with a bowed head. She was tired, thirsty and itchy in her new unwashed brocade shirt, but controlled herself to sit still. One by one the women came forward to lift her veil to look at her face, placing a coconut and a rupee plus a quarter as shagun in her lap with blessings for her husband's long life and begetting many sons. Some ran their fingers over the rich fabric of her brocade kameez, while others tried to guess the weight of her gold necklace.

"The girl has a narrow forehead and wheatish skin," quipped Sardar Naib Singh's massi, peering through her cataract afflicted eyes. She was still bristling from the rejection of her niece's match by Jeeti.

"Let it go behen ji, what will you do with a fair skin?" said Bhua. "Even nautch girls have good looks. Daughters-in-law should come from a good khandan, be obedient and serve you well."

"She has a good height though," remarked Bhindo from the neighbourhood.

Nimmo's trousseau was exhibited on jute string cots in the inner courtyard for all to see, evaluate and comment. Women surged around to see how many clothes, beddings, utensils and jewellery had been sent. Comparisons were made with all that had been received at Amaro's wedding. Silk shirts were felt between thumb and finger and jewellery pieces held up to estimate their weight. Embroidered phulkaris and bedsheets were appreciated.

"These bangles seem to be around eight tolas, Bhabi? You remember mine with the elephant faces? They are at least ten tolas if not more," said Amaro, critically examining a pair of gold bangles and tossing them in her hand. She was worried about the possibility of losing face in the family and the village if Nimmo's trousseau turned out to be better than hers. Women had surprisingly sharp memories of details of weddings held in the family over the years, and it came naturally to them to make candid comparisons of jewellery, clothes, articles and gifts brought by various family brides.

Jeeti handed out suits to women relatives along with turbans for their husbands, which Nimmo's family had sent as customary gifts for the boy's family and relatives. There were gifts of clothes and a gold kantha and murkian for Hukum Singh. Jeeti frowned—her son was not a village lout who would wear such ornaments! Neither was she happy with the two suits, a pair of gold bangles and a chain sent for her. Her sister had received a heavy gold set and four suits at her son's wedding. That slighted her position in front of her relatives. She remembered receiving a pair of gold earrings and bangles from Amaro's parents. There was a gold ring and kara for Sardar Naib Singh, but only a suit for Rano. Bhua sulked that she had been sent only a suit and no gold jewellery.

Sardar Naib Singh's massi smirked. "So is this all you are worth to your daughter-in-law's parents? They like to be known as big, moneyed sardars, but it doesn't seem so from the wedding. Had you accepted my niece they would have covered you in gold."

Hukum Singh sat in the men's quarters, enjoying a drinking party with his relatives and friends. It was a rowdy group with men getting drunk, quarrelling and arguing. Many found this a good opportunity to bring up old grudges and settle scores with each other.

Nimmo was taken to an inner room which she was to share with her sister-in-law Rano. She would not see much of her husband yet. It was not the custom for a groom and bride to interact when wedding guests were still around. Next morning, Jeeti took Nimmo and Hukum Singh to the village gurudwara for paying obeisance, offering karah parshad and praying to be blessed with a grandson!

Hukum Singh's family included his father Sardar Naib Singh, his mother Jeeti, his aged grandfather, a widowed Bhua and twenty-one-year-old sister Rano; his stepbrother Bachan Singh alias Bachana along with his wife Amaro and their children—a nine-year-old son Bheera and thirteen-year-old daughter Guddi. Jeeti, called Bebe by all younger members, was a fair, sharp-featured woman with a confident demeanour. She was the second wife of Sardar Naib Singh and younger to him by at least fifteen years. Bebe was the undisputed director of the household.

Sardar Naib Singh was the quintessential feudal landlord. In his late fifties, he was quite vain about his good looks and loved to twirl his luxuriant moustaches with his right thumb and forefinger every now and then. Overly particular about his appearance, his turbans and outfits had to be spotlessly clean and ironed. He wore a short sleeveless jacket called a vasket (a local rechristening of 'waistcoat') over a collared Boski shirt and narrow cut pyjamas, all of which were stitched by a famous tailor in Malerkotla. A pair of embroidered khussa with a large upturned toe made in the softest leather completed the attire. He enjoyed his shikar and social soirees with other Sardars and local officers, which included attending occasional dance performances by nautch girls. He enjoyed riding his dappled white mare and his evening peg with tandoori chicken, happy to leave petty household affairs to Jeeti and the farming to Bachana.

Sardar Naib Singh's elder son, Bachana, was born of his first wife who died when the young boy was six. Bachana had little resemblance to his fair and handsome father. Broad and swarthy with an overly hairy body and a hare lip, he had spent his childhood fighting other boys for being teased as 'Kalu', which was partly responsible for giving him a vitriolic disposition. A pair of thick eyebrows met over his dark beady eyes set in a narrow forehead, making him look perpetually angry. He had a bushy beard and moustache which camouflaged most of his face. In contrast to his father and brother, he had dark skin, which, according to Naib Singh's mother, resembled the bottom of an iron skillet, leading her to throw aspersions about his paternity upon her daughter-in-law.

"God only knows from whose seed this woman has conceived him. No one in our last three generations has been so dark or ugly! He certainly doesn't seem to be from our family!"

Bachana showed little interest in learning anything beyond the basic alphabet and could barely pull through the village madrassa. He often came home with a bloodied face from street brawls, and Sardar Naib Singh had to face people's complaints about his misbehaviour. His primary interest revolved around raising partridges and engaging them in public fights. Distilling liquor and inviting his friends to rowdy drink parties was another of his favourite pastimes. Sardar Naib Singh was a shrewd man and had assigned well thought out roles to both his sons. Bachana was given the entire responsibility of tending to the rough and tough work of farming and the farm animals while Hukum Singh was educated for a better station in life. It gave the fastidious Sardar a way of avoiding the menial work in agriculture, leaving him to live in style and move around at leisure attending weddings, obituaries and entertaining the local officers and others Sardars from the landed gentry. In return, he overlooked Bachana's boorish habits and let him indulge in his drinking and partridge fights. Hukum Singh was the preferred, pampered son who brought laurels to the family.

Bachana's wife Amaro was a homely, plump woman with no education and little finesse. Her eyes tended to dart around nervously and her round double-chinned face wore a constant anxious look as if in anticipation of some bad news. She had a compulsive habit of tugging her veil lower over her narrow forehead now and then as though it would be an unredeemable disaster if even a strand of her hair were to be revealed to the world. Most of her time was spent yelling at her son to do his schoolwork, at the risk of his father 'flaying him alive' and calling out for her daughter Guddi who was adept at escaping household tasks.

Rano came across as a pretty, sharp-featured, very light-complexioned girl till you noticed the squint in her left eye. She was very self-conscious about her defect and seemed to begrudge the world for it. Lazy and sullen, she got away by doing little in the house, except a bit of embroidery and weaving which gave her a chance to sit around and chat with other girls from the village. She was greatly troubled by the fact that all her friends had long been married, returning to their maternal homes to have babies, sometimes second ones. She was frequently afflicted with migraines and vague body aches and could be seen lying on the cot with a dupatta tied around her head. A young chamar girl, Bindo, who came in to clean the house and bathe the animals, was often summoned by her to press her head and massage her limbs. Jeeti had taken her to various hakims and soothsayers for sacred threads and magic potions, but nothing seemed to work. Sardar Naib Singh and Jeeti were seriously worried that Rano was crossing the marriageable age.

Sardar Naib Singh's elder sister, Bhua, addressed as such by the entire village, spent much of her time reading Gurbani and visiting the gurudwara, though not exclusively for spiritual pursuits. In a highly restrictive society which closely controlled women's movements, religion afforded one legitimate reason for an outing and socializing. Bhua was thin with a sharp nose and thin lips which gave her a somewhat dried-up, severe look. She mostly dressed in dun-coloured clothes and covered herself in a voluminous white chadar when stepping out of the house. It made her look sagacious and older than her actual age. Bhua seemed to know of everything that took place in the village and much that never did. She may not have thought much of her sister-in-law Jeeti, but was wise enough not to push her brother's goodwill too far. Sisters were given a place of respect in Punjab, and widows could claim full right to live with their brothers, as long as they behaved themselves and did not claim more than food, shelter and clothing.

Nimmo managed to catch a few hazy glimpses of Hukum Singh through the veil drawn low over her face.

What a handsome man he was! Standing tall with a broad chest that tapered down to a narrow waist, he had high cheek-bones, a sharp, chiselled nose and deep-set brown eyes. His sharp moustaches were groomed into an upward curl, and his beard tucked neatly into a net. He wore a meticulously wrapped maroon turban, with each fold in place in the army style. Hukum Singh smiled little, wearing a somewhat haughty expression. Even though Nimmo was only a shade darker than the average Punjabi girl, Hukum Singh's very fair skin made her appear dusky in comparison. She was in awe of him.

For the first four days Nimmo slept in the inner room with Rano, whereas the men slept in their individual baithaks across the courtyard. It would have been most unbecoming and shameless to have a new bride share her husband's room soon after marriage with the guests still around. Hukum Singh had only been granted a week's leave and would soon leave to join duty at Ambala. It took four days for all the wedding guests to leave for their respective villages and for Nimmo to meet Hukum Singh finally. The family finished an early dinner and started hauling their string cots to the roof when Amaro ushered her into Hukum Singh's room.

"This is where you sleep tonight. My brother-in-law is a sahib who is used to watching mems, pray that you come up to his expectations," she smirked at a nervous Nimmo.

Hukum Singh was well aware of his dapper looks and the fact that he was attractive to women. Wives of senior officers were extra kind to him and would pick out flimsy reasons to summon him. A couple of senior Indian officers with marriageable daughters had tried to send feelers to him. Hukum Singh could hardly explain to them the deep-rooted tribalism and parochialism in Jat Sikhs, who would not mess up their bloodline by marrying out of caste. Matches were, anyway, made by the parents, and it would be highly audacious to pick one's bride. Even if he had, how would he expect a city-bred girl to understand and adjust with his family and the rural component in his personality, which formed the core of every Jat? But like most men, when he imagined his future wife, he could not but help conjure up a face that reflected the charm and coquettishness of his favourite actress Naseem Banu, with large mesmerizing eyes and a fair, alabaster like face.

He had been dying to get a look at his wife. His heart-beat quickened with excitement when he saw her waiting, wrapped up in a pink veil. He removed the veil from her face with his heart beating fast in anticipation, uncovering a dusky face with beads of perspiration and smudged kohl. His bride sat in a loose, shapeless shirt and some tribal gold jewellery, her oily hair severely pulled back into a braid. His heart lurched with disappointment. She was not even close to the kind of wife he had imagined. Everything about her demeanour was rustic and lacking in style. He felt angry and resentful towards his mother and Bhua who had chosen this girl for him. Now he was trapped and must make the best of it. He tried to mask his disappointment make obligatory small talk, telling her that he must leave to join duty now and would send for her sometime later when he was allotted family quarters. Nimmo answered bashfully in nods and nervously waited for what would come next. No one had told her what to expect, and the only advice she had received was from her married cousin, who had directed her to make it hard for him to 'get her'.

"If you don't protest and fight, he will think you are too eager and will not let you rest later. So fight him when he tries to remove your clothes and push him away," she had said. What followed was unexpected and shocking for her unexposed sixteen years. She tried to fight Hukum Singh off, and he took it on as a project akin to breaking in a new mare, which made the experience worse for her. There was not much romance to their first night, and much soreness and bruises.

Next morning, Hukum Singh confronted Jeeti. "Bebe, is this the only hoorpari you could find for me in the whole of Punjab? She has neither looks nor education. How will I have her walk with me in my circle of officers? I will be the butt of jokes in my regiment."

"Calm down, son, she is very young, and will learn everything by and by. How many educated Jat girls can you find in Punjab? Did you want some oversmart girl to come and push you around? And it is not the girl alone that one has to consider, the family is a major concern too. There are still many things you do not understand."

Hukum Singh left for Ambala and Nimmo joined the women of the house in their daily chores. The day began early, as everyone woke up at the crack of dawn. Buffaloes were bathed, fed and milked, and the milk poured into large earthen pots which were placed in ovens dug into the ground and lighted with dung cakes. It was left to boil and simmer in these pots for long hours till it thickened to a reddish colour with a layer of thick cream on the top. Once it set as curds in the night, it would be churned to get butter and buttermilk the next morning. Handling the milk was done by Jeeti, who liked to control and dole out the good stuff herself; needless to say, the lion's share of the goodies went to the male members of the family, with leftovers for the daughters and daughters-in-law. An early breakfast of parantha, butter, curds and lassi was prepared for the men who would leave to work in the fields before the sun got too harsh.

Nimmo was careful to keep the veil drawn over her face until the men left home when she could safely lift it. Bau ji left much later to go and sit around in the village centre with other old men, playing cards and chatting, but the old chap was no longer considered virile or threatening enough to veil one's face from. He never forgot to carry some leftover rotis with him when he stepped out to feed birds and stray dogs in the streets. One could often see sparrows come and sit on his shoulder as he threw out little crumbs for them. Expectant street dogs waited for him to dole out bits of rotis.

"Bau ji, you keep stuffing your pockets with ghee-smeared rotis and stain your kurtas with grease. You just spoilt a new kurta yesterday, and the stains will not wash off. Do you think you alone are responsible for feeding the entire animal population of the village?" Jeeti admonished him.

"You ignorant woman, do these voiceless animals of God own fields which will feed them? Feeding them is a great act of charity which will help me in the next world," he replied patiently.

Jeeti was quick to take charge of all of Nimmo's jewellery and the expensive dresses she had brought along in her trousseau, on the pretext of keeping them safe. There was a row of small dark storage rooms known as kothris behind the large inner hall in the house, with no other opening except single, low doors. Some of these had large sandooks placed in them to store clothing, jewellery, beddings and money. The sandooks stood about six feet high and five feet broad, with several small windows opening in the front. They were quite a work of art, beautifully decorated with painted motifs and brass knobs and additions. Some of the kothris were used to store grain, molasses, ghee and other eatables. The keys to all the locks on these stores hung in a bunch tied to Jeeti's drawstring.

"I doubt that you will see your jewellery again," whispered Amaro. "She is trying to put together a trousseau for Rano."

"Surely they can afford to send their daughter with four ornaments of her own! I won't give mine," protested Nimmo.

"Things are not as prosperous as they seem here; the crop was really poor for the last two years, and the land dispute with Bapu ji's cousin from Jagadhari is draining money ceaselessly. They say you should not wish illness or court cases even for your enemy."

"Is Rano promised already?"

"The girl has bad stars; besides a sharp tongue, you must have noticed that she has a squint in her left eye; these things can hardly be hidden. That is why they are trying to lure someone with the promise of a fat trousseau."

Bheera and Guddi soon became very fond of Nimmo, and she would often play geete and stapu with Guddi, who was just three years younger to her. Both the children went to school, and often Nimmo would look wistfully at Guddi as she picked up her bag to be escorted to the village school nearby. She rued the fact that there was no school for girls in her village, and she had lost the opportunity to study further.

One day Nimmo stepped out to hang out her load of washed clothes on a rope stretched across the inner courtyard when she saw a banjara bangle seller hawking his wares in the street. He had a henna coloured beard trimmed short, long moustaches, a huge, lehriya turban, and a pair of silver murkian in his ears. Carrying his wares in two huge cloth bundles hung from the ends of a thick wooden stick placed over his shoulders, he called out to announce his arrival in a shrill, long drawn-out tone.

"Come and get exquisite seven-coloured bangles! Shiny glass bangles from Faizabad!"

Nimmo signalled for him to step into the courtyard and waited excitedly for the magic bundles to unveil their treasures. She called out to Amaro to join her. Guddi soon came running too and squatted alongside, chatting excitedly and waiting for the bundles to open. The bangle seller gingerly rested his bundles on the floor and squatted alongside. He proceeded to untie the knots with slow, studied movements, building up delightful expectation and curiosity. Rano and Bindo dropped whatever they were doing and joined them too. The banjara reached into his cloth bundle and drew out bunches of bangles in twinkling star-spangled blue, rich mustard golden, deep purple and verdant green. He seemed to have unleashed a whole rainbow of coquettish colours out of his bundle. As he held up each cluster of bangles for the women to admire, sun rays pierced the glass prisms, shooting sharp, shimmering hues on the brick wall behind. The women sat mesmerized, unable to take their eyes off the shiny bunches to decide which they liked more than the others. Ditti, the masseuse, who was passing by in the street, saw the bangle seller and stepped in to join the small circle of women and girls.

"So you are buying new bangles, daughter-in-law? It seems Hukum is coming to fetch you!" she laughed. "Massi," she called out to another woman crossing the street, "Come in and see the bangles daughter-in-law is buying!"

Soon there was a small cluster of excited women and girls squatting around the bangle seller, peering into and touching the magical, twinkling, multi-coloured bunches of Faizabadi bangles.

Ditti pointed towards a set of sunny yellow bangles. "Try these mustard-flower coloured bangles, bahu."

"Oh no, these will look good only on fair arms. Go for these rose-coloured ones," said Amaro.

Guddi wistfully reached out for the sky-blue and purple coloured bangles and looked pleadingly at her mother. "Get these for me, Bebe."

Amaro slapped her hand aside.

"Don't go and break them now. Why do you want these just yet? Have we settled your engagement for next month?"

Despite of the various suggestions, Rano took time making up her mind about which bangles to choose. She finally settled for a set of deep green bangles with specks of gold dust on them, moving her arm around to see them shimmer. Amaro picked up pink ones with blue stripes. Rano sulked that none were too good for her, but bought some golden ones anyway. Nimmo bought some for Guddi, making her jump for joy. Even though the rest of the women did not buy any bangles, they derived great pleasure from looking at them, touching and experiencing the colour and shine, the bold brightness and shy tinkle of the rich collection of colour and glass.

The bangle seller urged the women to get their names tattooed on their arms. Nimmo was adventurous and wanted to try everything that women do to make themselves pretty for their men.

"Will it hurt much?" she asked hesitatingly.

"You will not find anyone who does it better in the whole region, Biba ji. I have an experience of twenty years. You will feel nothing more than a mosquito bite and it will be over before you know it. What is your name?"

"Nimmo," she said, extending her arm. She clenched her teeth and shut her eyes tight to contain the pain as the banjara pricked her skin to stain it with blue dye. What a lot of mosquito bites for heaven's sake!

"Go ahead and open your eyes, Biba ji. Look what a beautiful name I have written for you!" said the bangle seller, applying some pungent oil on the tattoo.

Nimmo opened her eyes to look at her arm. She was startled to see long, sweeping Urdu alphabets etched on her forearm.

"Hai, hai, why have you written my name in Urdu? I can't even read it," she exclaimed.

"That is the only language I know, Biba ji, I have

written 'Nimmo'. There, now you can read it."

Anyway, it was done now and even though she could not read Urdu, the flowing letters looked pretty and decorative. Many times that day she moved her wrists to catch the light in her bangles and imagined Hukum Singh's reaction to the pretty picture they made. It made her forget the throbbing pain in her tattooed arm.

6

Birds in a Cage

The winter sun soaked the courtyard in its benevolent warmth. Wisps of smoke rose from the clay oven dug into the ground in the corner and fired with cow dung cakes. Dal simmered in a clay pot in the oven giving out a delicious aroma. Children sat on string cots stripping long sugar cane sticks with their teeth and sucking on the sticky, sweet juice. Nimmo and Amaro sat on low peerhis making sewian (vermicelli) by rolling little bits of wheat flour dough between the thumb and forefinger and spreading them out on a cloth sheet to dry in the sun till they were crisp. A popular Punjabi sweet dish, sewian were fried and cooked in milk and jaggery and served topped with dry fruit and sultanas.

A black crow alighted on the boundary wall and crowed raucously. Amaro quickly waved her arm to shoo it away before it could swoop down for a mouthful of the dough. Nimmo looked at it with a shy smile and said, "Don't scare it away, Behenji. He might be heralding a visit from someone."

"Do you think of anything else but your husband all day?" asked Amaro. "That's why you let the milk boil over today morning. This kind of intoxication of a new wedding lasts for a while only. You soon start to see the true colours of men. They will be nice to you in the beginning, but before you know, the drinking and beating will start. Don't hope for too much from your husband—they do not care for wives; men only need them and use them for their comfort."

A bicycle bell tinkled in the narrow lane outside the house gate. The postman called out:

"Letter ji!"

Nimmo curbed her impulse to rush out and grab the letter.

"Bheere go and get the letter."

Bheera smiled mischievously as he skipped past her, waving the letter.

"Bebe, there is a letter from Chacha."

Bebe Jeeti left her spinning and hurriedly stepped out of the room into the courtyard.

"Read it aloud, son."

Nimmo strained her ears to hear every word that Bheera read out haltingly, lest she miss out on something.

"Dear Bapu ji, I touch your feet. I am in good spirits and health and wish the same for all of you from Waheguru. What is the latest about the court case with Jagadhari-wale Sardar? Has the boori buffalo delivered a calf yet? I hope the sugarcane crop is good this year. Ask

Bebe to make some pinnis for me. I am sending a money order for buying some gold for Rano's wedding. I am hopeful of getting family quarters soon. I will get some leave shortly and come home. Convey my Sat Sri Akal to all and love to the children. I bow to Bebe and Bapu ji. Your obedient son, Hukum Singh."

"May my Sarwan son live for centuries! Waheguru's blessings be on him!" Jeeti beamed after grabbing the money order.

Nimmo consoled herself that the 'Sat Sri Akal to all' held a special one for her; no man would be audacious enough to send a separate letter to his newlywed wife or even make an overt mention of her. She gave an extra affectionate pat to the pet dog Kalu, her heart leaping at the news that Hukum Singh would soon get family quarters and she would be able to join him in Ambala.

Days passed as she tried to keep her mother-in-law happy and counter the power games of her sisters-in-law Rano and Amaro, both of whom could not disguise their resentment that Nimmo would eventually leave the village to join Hukum Singh and live independently in a city. Jeeti quite forgot that she was barely over sixteen and often chided her for playing with Guddi or letting the veil slip from her head.

"Better start saluting our Nimmo now, Bebe; she is going to become a memsahib soon! Look at a woman like me, who will spend her entire life sweeping and cooking and tending to animals. It's all one's destiny," said Amaro.

"It's all one's luck, Bhabi," replied Rano churlishly. "God only knows what good deeds she has done which we have not. It's not even that she is a Heer or Sohni!"

"Don't let it turn your head girl," said Jeeti. "Remember Hukum is my son and you are fortunate to marry him and get such a good life which most girls can only dream of. May Waheguru come to the aid of my daughter too and find her a good husband. Now hurry up and finish making this vermicelli. There is so much more work to be done. You really are slow with your hands. And you, Amaro, control your tongue and stop ruing your fate. To listen to you, one would think you have come from some royal family where women sit with henna on their feet all day."

One evening, Nimmo lifted an earthen milk pot from the oven, not realizing how hot it was. She scorched her hands, and the earthen pot fell and smashed into many pieces, with the milk flowing all over the ground. Milk was the most precious commodity and had to be handled carefully.

"Hai hai, why are you bent upon destroying things in my house, useless girl? Did your mother not even teach you how to do basic chores? You have neither looks nor talent." Jeeti slapped Nimmo and let off a series of abuses targeting her mother and poor upbringing.

Amaro and Rano enjoyed the spectacle of a humiliated Nimmo sobbing into her veil. Being the youngest daughter-in-law, Nimmo was not allowed to step out in the village without a chaperone. So there was no friend that she could confide in to lighten her heart. None of the younger women from wealthy families went out much unless there was a wedding or death in the neighbourhood. Women mostly went out in pairs or groups, a maid being sent first to announce their visit.

Nimmo missed her home and family and she pined for

her sister Bholan who had seemed such a nuisance with her constant quarrels. Now she would have given anything to go and hug her. How she wished she could lean her head against her mother's shoulder and complain to her. She missed her best friends Sakina, Baggi and Tipi, imagining them playing stapu and swinging under the old pipal tree near the mosque, going to the bhatti to get maize roasted in the sand and munching it with sticky jaggery. Much as she tried to push it out of her head, Akhtar's smiling face would flash in her mind every time she felt low. But that was a different life, and this was another; there was no going back. Her mother's words came back to her—daughters do not belong to their parents, who have a limited role of being their guardians till they are ready to go to their husband's homes, which is their true home.

There was another reason for Nimmo's loneliness. She was a full-blooded girl in the first flush of youth, and having newly tasted the thrill of sex, her body pained and hungered for physical satiation. She found herself twisting and turning in her bed at night, feverish and restless with a searing desire. Her mind replayed her lovemaking with Hukum Singh over and over again, trying to relive the thrill. She seldom had a role to play in their lovemaking, the entire process being orchestrated to pleasure her husband. But the pleasures of the flesh set her on fire and her eager young body responded fast. Sometimes, as she lay sleepless trying to fantasize a way to quench the fierce fires in her body, it was Akhtar's face and body which merged with her own rather than Hukum Singh's. He kissed her tenderly, played with her hair, stroked her body languidly, said sweet nothings to her; he did not hurry through the rough motions of reaching his satisfaction to roll over and sleep. She felt guilty and tried to censor her mind from forbidden fantasies, but when have minds ever given in to censorship?

The weather turned chilly, and people could be seen huddled around small bonfires, wrapped in shawls. As the sugar cane crop was harvested, large fire pits were dug in the ground to make jaggery. Cane juice was extracted and poured into huge iron skillets placed over large fire pits, boiled and stirred constantly with long iron ladles till it reduced to a thick, muddy, brown mass. It was a precise process carried out by trained men; one mistake could spoil the entire lot. Small mounds of hot jaggery were laid out on a cloth sheet to be dried and stored in large earthen pots. Nimmo loved the dollops of warm, freshly made jaggery that melted in one's mouth. She decided to walk down to the field and get some for herself. Nimmo was carefully balancing her footsteps on the narrow raised mud bank on the periphery of the field to keep from slipping into the wet mud and happily sucking on fresh jaggery when she was startled to hear a sharp rebuke from behind her and nearly lost her balance.

"Have you no shame at all, moving around in front of unknown men with a naked face? Is this your parent's village that you have stepped outside without a ghagra and a chadar?" said Bachana.

Coming up close to her, Bachana grasped her at the upper arms and glared down at her. He was close enough for her to feel his breath on her face. His deep-set eyes glinted as he looked fixedly at her, sending a shiver through her body. Unable to move away, Nimmo lowered her tear-stung eyes, burning with humiliation. They were only farmworkers! Wouldn't she trip over and fall flat if she couldn't see where she was going? She had noticed Bachana ogle at her more than once when he thought no one was looking. He often found a pretext to come home whenever she was alone and demand tea or lassi, trying to find reasons to make small talk with her. But he was also kind to her and would make sure that whenever he brought some sweets for the family, she got her share. He had brought a new suit from the city for Amaro last month, and gave her one too, which did not go down too well with his wife. Nimmo was young, naïve, easily pleased and thankful for these small gestures. Bachana often enjoyed a drink too many resulting in drunken assaults on Amaro at night. The family chose to ignore her stifled cries. What happened between man and wife was no one else's business.

Bachana had an intriguing hobby. He kept a pair of partridges and tended to them with great care. The household would rise to the sharp 'tee...tee...tee' calls of the freckled, dun-coloured birds in the morning, and Bachana would go up to their cage on the rooftop to feed them. He took great pride in pitching them for fights with partridges of other hobbyists from neighbouring villages. A partridge fight was a much-awaited event in the village and would be announced to the villagers from the rooftop a couple of days in advance. The beginning of winter was a good time for bird fights, summer being the breeding season.

One such tournament was held on the second day of Assu, the seventh day of the Nanakshahi calendar. The air was refreshingly crisp, and winter dripped sweetness into sugarcane fields. Villagers gathered slowly in the open space near the pond for the match. A large number of men from nearby villages also flocked to Raipur to watch the tournament, and soon there was quite a crowd. Some sat on their haunches and shared village news, while others stood around in groups. An excited murmur went up in the gathering as Bachana arrived with his lackeys holding a partridge cage covered with cloth. Today the tournament was to be with Sukhram's birds, a farmer from the village of Rayya. He was known to boast that no one had yet defeated his partridges Gama and Bheem, and the spectators were eager to test his claim. The air was thick with anticipation and excitement as both men took their places in the centre of the circle. People's eyes were fixed on the cloth-covered cages in their hands.

Bachana and Sukhram removed the coverings from the cages and let the birds out. There was a flutter of feathers as the partridges preened and blinked their eyes in the sunlight. Those who would bet money on the winner craned their necks to get a good look at the birds and placed their bets.

"Shabaash, Heere, this is your day. Don't let my back touch the ground, my lion!" said Bachana, stroking the bird's back.

"No one can beat you Gama, my son. Show everyone your strength today!" said Sukhram, holding up his bird for all to see.

The birds had been starved and subsequently given a purgative the day before to cleanse their system and make them alert and agile. Their beaks had been sharpened with a penknife to lacerate the opponent's head. A large flat place was cleared for the fight, and grain sprinkled on the arena. Held by their owners at the opposite ends, the birds were exhibited to the audience before being set against each other with encouraging shouts.

The partridges picked up the excitement from the whistles, catcalls and whoops, fluffed out their bodies to the maximum and fluttered their wings in a frenzy. Focused on the opponent, they circled and took tense, low flights before clashing blindly over and over again in a cloud of dust and feathers and screeching. The crowd craned their necks and bodies in a mass of collective, throbbing expectation of culmination of a feverish, primal urge. Shouts and cheering went up every time the birds clashed, as the onlookers urged and shouted for the birds they had bet on, goading them to draw blood.

"Take him on! Go for him!"

"Ho! Ho! Tear him apart now!"

"Attack my lion, attack! Don't leave him!"

"Shabaash! Nail him, son!"

The fight continued for twenty minutes before one of the birds turned tail and ran out of the circle, leaving a trail of blood behind him. It was Bachana's bird. Sukhram's partridge had his beak smeared with blood. A roar of cheering went up in the crowd, and Sukhram and his cronies broke out in victorious ululation. Bachana's face turned a thunderous black as he marched away sullenly, leaving his helpers to bring back the injured bird. The bettors collected their money, and the crowd started dispersing, getting back to their fields and homes.

Sardar Naib Singh watched Bindo move around the house doing her daily chores. A young girl of about eighteen, Bindo was the daughter of Natha chamar, who worked as a field hand on Sardar Naib Singh's land. Being unmarried, she was not expected to cover her face in front of males. Not pretty in the classic sense, Bindo was nevertheless attractive for the sheer charm of youth. She had a spring to her step, and her supple, full-fleshed body moved with a wild animal's untamed grace. Her thick lips mostly remained slightly open, and she often smiled for no reason at all, a habit born out of constant servility. Her father worried about her marriage, but they were poor, and she had five younger siblings to be fed. Her mother had earlier worked for the Sardar's first wife, but Bindo replaced her after she contracted TB. Sardar ji had been very generous by giving them money for her treatment, and she tried to serve the family to the best of her ability.

One evening, the women had gone to attend a wedding in the village and Bachana was away with his cronies. Bau ji had retired to his room. Bindo was preparing to leave after finishing up with some housework when Sardar Naib Singh called out to her to bring him a glass and water for his drink.

"How old are you?" He asked, pouring whiskey into the glass.

"I am not sure," replied Bindo shyly, "Ma says I was born during the great floods, and so may be eighteen or nineteen years."

"Your father is worried about your marriage. Your youth is passing by. Soon it may be difficult to find a groom for you. And then there is all the expenditure on your mother's illness."

Bindo kept quiet and looked down at her bare toes.

"Let me see how I can help you. Come and massage my legs. I am tired."

Bindo sat down at his feet and started massaging his legs as he sipped his whiskey. The touch of her young hands on his calves sent an electric thrill through his body. Her shirt was torn over one shoulder, and she had kept it covered with her dupatta. The dupatta slipped as she bent to massage his legs, baring her skin. Sardar Naib Singh slowly ran his hands over her bare skin and got up to latch the door.

"I will buy you many new clothes, girl."

Bindo looked at him like a trapped doe, saying nothing.

It was late when the women returned from the wedding, and Jeeti and Amaro went inside the women's quarters to lay out the beds. Nimmo lagged to collect some clothes that had been spread out to dry when she saw a person slip out of Sardar Naib Singh's baithak and move towards the gate.

"Who goes there? Stop, whoever you are," she shouted, running towards the silhouette in the semi-darkness. She caught up with the woman just as she was rushing out of the gate, and was shocked to see Bindo, her hair and clothes in disarray.

"Bindo? You were supposed to leave when we left. What were you doing here so late in Bapu ji's room?" she asked.

"Bhabi ji, he kept me back to massage his legs. We survive on the morsels of his charity. How could I refuse him?" Bindo covered her face with her dupatta and broke down sobbing.

Shocked and disgusted, Nimmo could hardly sleep that night. She knew this was a sensitive issue, but could not keep it to herself either. Next morning she told Amaro about it.

"The horny old bastard!" she exclaimed. "But what else do you expect from Sardars? They think it is their right to savour the chamar women! How ironic that these untouchable women whom the uppity Jattis shoo away from their hallowed kitchens share their husbands' beds! You see all those fair-skinned chamars with sharp noses and chiselled features? Many of them have been sired by Jat men. It's better to keep quiet about this and not mention it to anyone. You think Bebe is not aware of his habits? What can women do anyway? It is their destiny to tolerate their malik's adventures and turn a blind eye. Men will be men, after all."

A buffalo lowed in the backyard. Tethered to a stake, it waited to be fed, generously offering an abundant supply of milk to the master who owned her. Nimmo tried to make peace with the fact that men had many rights which were not to be mentioned or questioned by the women.

7

Mantra Tantra

Monsoon was a welcome season for the sun-scorched fields and dried up nullahs thirsting for water. Huge, rumbling black clouds would suddenly roar across the skies, sending everyone scurrying to secure things against the impending deluge. Animals were moved under shelters; women covered earthen chullahs with tin sheets, securing them with bricks to keep them from flying off. Clothes hung out to dry were hurriedly snatched from clotheslines, and string cots dragged into rooms. Mud roofs leaked profusely, and people rushed around placing pots and pans to catch the dripping rainwater. Muddy rainwater splashed into courtyards through tin spouts inserted in roofs. Naked children splashed and romped gleefully in rivulets of water flowing through the village lanes. Women hurried to finish the evening meal early to avoid swarms of winged insects which emerged from nowhere to hover around hurricane lanterns in the evening.

Rano paced up and down the courtyard, complaining of a headache. Kalu received an undeserved whack from her and ran away whimpering. The rainy season aggravated her restlessness and agitation. She had been praying and fasting for her marriage since long; it was humiliating when visiting female relatives looked at her with pity, clucked their tongues and enquired about her prospects. She began doubting that anyone would accept her with her defect, and it made her frustrated and bitter. She would soon be touching twenty-two. Most of her friends were already returning home to have their second or third child. She could hardly bear to meet them. It was infuriating to have relatives suggest matches of old, widowed or previously married men for her. In pedigreed families like hers, it was unacceptable to marry below one's station, though marrying off a daughter to a much older wealthy widower or married man was quite acceptable. Rano felt a seizure coming on once again. She fell onto a cot, flailing her arms wildly and making muffled sounds. Her eyes rolled up to show the whites.

"Hurry and fetch some water, Amaro. Nimmo, rub her feet with mustard oil," said Jeeti, fanning her face.

Rano thrashed her legs and rolled and twisted her body. Amaro tried to pour some water through her tightly clenched teeth. Nimmo, who was trying to rub her feet with oil, was hit hard by her thrashing foot and hurriedly stepped aside. Bimla, the cleaner woman, picked up a jutti and rubbed it on her nose.

"Smelling an old jutti is a sure shot remedy for dandal, Bibi ji," she said.

A few other women had stepped in from the street after hearing the commotion and heartily agreed with Bimla's suggestion.

"Bibi Jinns are often known to possess unmarried girls. You should take her to a sayaana," suggested another.

"It is definitely a spirit that has got into her," agreed the nain.

Roaming ascetics and sadhus often camped at the village for some days, and people welcomed them to listen to kirtan and religious discourses. A group of children playing in the street excitedly announced the arrival of a sadhu in Raipur. Women left what they were doing to peer out of their doors. It was soon a talk around the village that this was a very holy and charismatic sadhu from Hemkund, who could cure people of serious illnesses merely by giving them parshad and stroking their head. The sadhu and his attendants settled in an old haveli on the outskirts of the village, and people started to visit him with offerings of jaggery, flour or money. They went to him with myriad needs, hopes and aspirations; to heal their ailments, to wean their sons away from alcohol or hashish, and to help them win ongoing court cases for land disputes. Women asked for sons, grooms for their daughters, attention from neglectful husbands, and delivery from the tyranny of their mothers-in-law.

Jeeti took Rano with her to the sadhu to seek his blessings. Baba Mast ji sat cross-legged on a cot, facing a congregation of devout villagers. Fair and well-built, the young Baba was dressed in a white kurta and dhoti, with a flowing beard and thick open hair touching his shoulders. A long vermilion tikka adorned his forehead. He sat with his eyes shut, wearing a rudraksha mala in his neck and running a rosary through his fingers. His attendants stood behind him, waving a fan over his head. The gathering of villagers sat patiently, waiting their turn to speak to the Baba. His impressive personality overawed Jeeti.

"Just look how his forehead glows! One can see from afar what a divine soul he is. Maybe Waheguru has sent him specially to put an end to our problem. Bow down to him, daughter. He may be your saviour."

Jeeti and Rano prostrated themselves at the Baba's feet reverently and handed over a cash offering to his attendant sitting on the side. Baba Mast ji, as people were told, did not touch money at all. His attendants, of course, accepted it only to be used for serving the needy. The Baba opened his eyes after some time and recited a shloka which no one understood; nevertheless, everyone present was impressed by his knowledge of the scriptures and joined their hands in reverence. He took a long, intense look at the gathering, and pointed out at a mother holding a young, sickly, whimpering child.

"Bibi, bring this child here. Does he keep unwell?"

The woman scampered to go and bow at his feet and put her child forward.

"Yes maharaj, you know it all. He has been ill for the last month, and nothing seems to work. Please bless him and make him well."

Baba Mast ji shut his eyes and sprinkled some water over the screaming child's head, mumbling incoherently. Taking a handful of almonds from a bowl, he blew over them and gave them to the woman.

"Recite Om with a sincere heart and feed him one each

morning after sunrise and he will be fine."

"But Baba ji, the child has not teethed yet. How will he chew almonds?" asked the woman.

The Baba seemed flummoxed for a moment.

"Foolish woman, crush them first."

Sukha chamar came forward to request for help in an ongoing feud with his relative from the neighbouring village.

"Feed this parshad to your enemy, and his heart will be cleansed of all malice and anger towards you," said the Baba, handing him some patasas.

"Baba ji, he will probably break open my head before I get within ten feet of him. What good will the parshad do to me after that?"

An old man hobbled forward, asking for a cure for his arthritis. He was given some oil to rub on his joints. Many people consulted Baba Mast ji before Jeeti and Rano could avail their turn. The Baba looked at Rano, and turned to ask Jeeti, "So you are having difficulty finding a groom for this girl?"

Her faith further strengthened by the Baba's insight, an overwhelmed Jeeti held his feet and whispered, "Baba ji, you know everything without being told. Please help us. We are at your mercy now. I am ready to do whatever you tell me."

He looked hard and long at Rano.

"The girl is under the malicious influence of Shani. Shani cannot be tackled in the presence of the sun. Bring her to us after sunset today, and we will see what we can do."

Full of gratitude, Jeeti and Rano both bowed to his feet

and left.

"Baba Mast ji seems to have been sent by God specially to solve my problems. He could know my troubles without my having to tell him. This is the mark of holy men. They can read one's mind. And look at the glow on his face! One can hardly bear to look into his eyes for the light in them!"

Jeeti could not stop singing praises of Baba's unusual powers and asked Nimmo to accompany them to his camp too.

"Look at you. Two seasons have passed since your marriage, and you are still roaming around empty-handed. My niece got married much after you, and she has a son playing in the house. May be Baba ji's blessings will bring a son to your lap too."

Rano cooked some halwa to take as an offering for Baba Mast ji, and the three women reached his camp at sunset. His attendant asked them to wait in the outer room as Baba ji was in meditation. Another follower chanted a hymn, asking everyone to sing after him.

"The Baba ji is in communion with the Master, and we must wait till he comes out of the trance."

A quarter-of-an-hour later, the women were half dozing when an attendant came to summon Rano. Others were to wait outside. Rano followed the attendant and Jeeti promptly dozed off again. Another quarter-of-an-hour passed; curiosity got the better of Nimmo and she quietly crept up to peek into the room through a chink in the old wooden door. She was shocked at what she saw. Rano lay supine on the mat with her shirt raised over her body while the Baba bent over her, caressing her bare body with his hands. She pushed opened the door and rushed in.

"Hai hai! What is this you are doing, Baba ji?"

Taken by surprise, the Baba made a great show of anger.

"Foolish girl, how dare you come in and disturb my ritual? You will bring ruin on yourself by your lack of faith in a saint. The Shani has a hold on her. I was trying to purify this unfortunate girl through a mantar. You have no idea about my powers. Now you alone will be responsible for all the ills that will befall her and your family!"

Rano raved and ranted about Nimmo's sacrilege to save face with her mother. Denied any outlet for youthful urges, she had quite enjoyed the young Baba's attention and was embarrassed and resentful of Nimmo's unwelcome interruption. Jeeti sided with her daughter and admonished Nimmo for disturbing the Baba's healing and incurring his wrath. Thereafter, Nimmo became a frequent target of Rano's pent up anger.

"Hai…what have you done with the halwa Nimmo, no one ever makes it at your parents' house, I suppose?"

Jeeti and Amaro were quick to join in scoffing her: "If you have any illusion of superiority for being a Zaildar's daughter, you better get rid of it." Nimmo bit her tongue and kept quiet. Her time would come. She poured some halwa into a baati and took it for Bau ji. Dressed in a kurta, a loose white cloth tied around the waist, and a white turban draped around his head, the old man sat in the sun on his chair on the raised brick platform in front of the 'haveli'. Most of his day was spent answering salutations of passer-byes and throwing scraps of rotis to dogs and birds. He blessed Nimmo with a creased, toothless smile as she handed him the halwa.

"May your husband and brothers live long, daughter-in-law; they do not often remember to give delicacies to this old man."

Increasingly worried about her daughter's matrimonial prospects, Jeeti followed all kinds of superstitious rituals suggested by the village pandit. An itchy, black street dog struck luck every Friday when Rano fed it milk, and the sweeper woman was delighted when presented with a suit on massya. Jeeti made several trips to meet and request her relatives to search for a suitable match for Rano. The nai had been summoned many times for suggestions. Sardar Naib Singh felt that they had no option but to accept a widower or previously married man for her, but Jeeti could not bring herself to agree. Who knew the pain of being the second wife better than her? She came from a poor farmer's family who had seven daughters to be married off. Naib Singh was looking for a second wife as his first wife was ill with tuberculosis and banished to the outer quarters of the house. Naib Singh had one son by her, who needed to be raised too. So Jeeti, fifteen years his junior, came to the house as his second wife. She was put in charge of a ten-year-old foul-mouthed, rebellious Bachana and expected to nurse Naib Singh's ailing wife, who died after four years of Jeeti's marriage. Bachana never accepted her as a mother and remained resentful and belligerent. Jeeti was not much of a mother to him either, taking him on as an unpleasant duty. She soon had her own children, and neglected him for the most part.

"Are you aware that Guddi is almost of age to be married too? How long will you keep sitting with a girl as high as a camel in your house? People have started remarking about it. And the shameless girl lounges around most of the time with Bindo caressing her legs and arms! I will not wait much longer now," said Sardar Naib Singh.

Rano had often heard her mother recount her miseries when she came as a second wife, and announced that she would kill herself if given as a second wife to an older man. Jeeti was caught between practicality and sentiments. Sardar ji was right, but she could not bring herself to push her daughter into the same hopeless situation that she had endured. She asked him to give her one last chance; if she could not fix a match for Rano by the end of Magh, he was free to take the second option.

Another season passed as Nimmo milked buffaloes, cooked saag and washed clothes. She carried on with the hope that this phase would pass and she would soon be with her husband. Many a time she would toss and turn on her bed at night, conjuring up Hukum Singh's sinewy arms around her. Every time someone passing by through the street stopped at the gate, she would expectantly look up to see if it was the postman. Hukum Singh would occasionally arrive unannounced for short visits, though he did not seem to find much time for her. It was, anyhow, deemed shameless for a husband and wife to even speak to each other in front of elders. His days were spent visiting the fields with his father and meeting friends and relatives in the village. She mostly got to see him only in bed at night. There was not much communication between them besides a quick, matter of fact lovemaking session followed by Hukum Singh's snoring. Nimmo was much in awe of him to say anything, and her occasional timid questions were answered briefly. There were times when he was in a good mood and told her about his achievements in sports and the amazing lifestyles of the white officers; about glittering mess parties, hunting trips and training adventures in Hardwar. His accounts left her mesmerized, and she listened to him with great wonder. In his last visit, he had brought some imported chocolates for her from the canteen, and she had screwed up her nose at the first bite. The chocolate had tasted like sweet soap to her!

"I forgot that you have no taste for such things; you should stick with laddoo and jalebi," Hukum Singh had remarked with a disdainful smirk, reminding her of her ignorance and lack of sophistication.

Finally, Hukum Singh came home to announce that he had been allotted family quarters. Concerned about her son being fed poor food in the mess, Jeeti told Nimmo to get ready to accompany him to Ambala. Nimmo was overjoyed. After many hugs and some ceremonial sobbing, Nimmo stepped out to follow her husband towards a much-awaited, exciting new period in her life.

8

Akhtar

Akhtar had learnt and imbibed much from his father, Mian Ali Beg, a progressive and aware man. A member of the village panchayat, he was respected for his sagaciousness and helpfulness. Mian had stepped in to take on the marriage expenses for Bhikka mazbhi's daughter last summer and helped rebuild Attari's hut which had been swept away by the rains. Many other villagers were beholden to him for help and support on various occasions. Though Mian had not studied beyond the village Madrassa, he was a self-educated man through his love of reading. The greater part of his mornings was dedicated to reading newspapers, giving him enough fodder to debate current affairs with his sons and friends later in the evening.

Akhtar was a bright boy who excelled both in studies and extracurricular activities. He was the president of the college student union and popular amongst his circle of friends. Consumed by his involvement in the freedom movement, he did not find much time or inclination to pay attention to girls. But Nimmo stayed safe in some hidden corner of his heart, her memories often resurfacing like parts of a lost dream. He would wait to hear bits and pieces of news about her from his mother and sister Sakina. She seemed to be happy in her new life as a memsahib.

"Akhtar son, have you considered your khala's proposal about her daughter Amina?" asked his mother Hajjo. "She is a pretty, obedient girl and well known to us all. We must give them an answer. You have turned down so many offers that now people are wary of even suggesting a match for you. Relatives have started thinking that we have our nose up in the air. Tell me exactly what kind of girl you want."

"Ammi, it's not that I am looking for a hoorpari. I am just too busy with more important issues than marriage right now. How can I think of myself when the very future of our country is at stake? The call of the hour is for each one of us to step out of our personal concerns and focus our energies on one goal only—an independent and undivided India."

"Let the boy live, Hajjo." said Mian Ali Beg, lowering his newspaper and peeking over the rim of his spectacles. "He is not going grey or bald in the near future, I assure you. It is better that we worry about Sakina first."

"Of course, let us wait till he is bald and then we can pair him up with Jeoni Tai who has lost all her teeth!" laughed Hajjo.

"I have invited Ahmed over for tea today. I have a feeling that he and Sakina like each other," said Mian.

"Hai Allah! What are you saying? Don't you know they are Shias? What will our biradari say? We will be socially boycotted!" exclaimed Hajjo.

"I care more about my girl's happiness than the biradari. And you are well aware that I do not believe in these differences at all. Did Allah make Shias and Sunnis separately in heaven? He is a well-settled boy with a good reputation. My daughter likes him. That is all that is important," replied Mian.

"I agree with Abba ji," said Akhtar. "We should not allow such meaningless social barriers to stand in the way of Sakina's happiness. Ahmed is a fine young man. My only problem with him is that he is a blind follower of Jinnah. But he is Sakina's choice, so I am happy about it. And Ammi, All India Azad Muslim Conference has organized a protest march against the Lahore Resolution in Ludhiana tomorrow. You and the girls must come with us too."

"What is this about? Is it not enough that you three men are going? Why must you take the young girls and me along? People will talk," said Hajjo.

"To answer your first question: Jinnah's party The All India Muslim League is pushing for a division of the country based on the Two-Nation Theory which sees Hindus and Muslims as two distinct nations who cannot live together in peace and harmony. The Hindu Maha Sabha led by Lala Lajpat Rai thinks likewise and dreams of a Hindu Rashtra. The All India Azad Muslim party, along with many other organizations, is fighting tooth and nail to stop the vivisection of Hindustan. Those who sit back and allow the power mongers to tear this nation apart will have to answer to posterity for a huge wrong which will never be righted again."

"Hai hai, who says Hindus and Muslims cannot live together in peace and harmony? I agree I have had some quarrels with the Panditani and the next door Sito, but we sorted them out soon enough. No one will leave one's home and village over such petty issues, surely?" asked Hajjo.

Waseem and Mian Ali Beg laughed and called out to Sakina and Shammi to join them.

"Girls, tomorrow we are all going to Ludhiana to join a protest march against the Lahore Resolution. Be ready at eight."

"Bhai jaan has already told us all about it," replied Sakina enthusiastically.

"I hope the police won't catch us and put us in jail, Abba ji?" asked thirteen-year-old Shammi.

"Well, you are the biggest revolutionary posing the greatest threat to the British Empire right now, so I can guarantee nothing," teased Akhtar.

"Bhai jaan, I also oppose the devastating Two-Nation Theory, which will drive people away from their homes and hearths, and has no justification in a multicultural and multi-religious country like India," said Sakina. "But I feel you are unfair to hold Jinnah alone responsible for it. Don't forget that V.D. Savarkar, the chief patron of Sangh Parivar, formulated this concept in his 1923 essay 'Hindutva' sixteen years before Jinnah propagated it. The Hindu Mahasabha, Lala Lajpat Rai, Pandit Madan Mohan Malviya, all have put the Hindu interests over and above those of Hindustan as a composite unit. They even refused to join the Quit India movement. Even though

Gandhi and Nehru have been opposing partition, they are insistent on a centralized federal structure, arousing a sense of insecurity in the Muslim League."

"I am so glad you are keeping yourself aware of the goings-on, Sakina. I am sure your discussions with Ahmed are also immensely helpful in furthering your knowledge about the various political updates," teased Akhtar.

"All that is very well, but better leave these issues to the men," said Hajjo. "Women's place is in the house with their children. Does it look nice that they should walk with unknown men in the streets carrying banners and raising slogans?"

"Begum, I must remind you that hundreds of Muslim women have fought and even given their lives for the freedom of our country," replied Mian Ali Beg. "Saadat Bano Kitchlew, wife of Dr Saifuddin Kitchlew, Zulekha Begum, wife of Maulana Azad, Mehr Taj, daughter of Khan Abdul Ghaffar Khan to name only a few. How are women any less capable of resistance than men? Look at the world over, only cultures where men and women have worked together have prospered and moved forward. If half of the population is shackled and made unproductive to serve as domestic minions, the country will always lag behind others in every way."

Waseem clanked the heavy door chain on the main door and ushered Ahmed inside the house. Sakina and Shammi went indoors while Ahmed was welcomed and seated by Mian and Akhtar. Ahmed worked in a managerial position in one of the hosiery factories in Doraha. Of an average build and ordinary looks, Ahmed was nevertheless a pleasant-looking young man. He had dressed with extra care in a pair of blue pants and check shirt to meet his prospective in-laws, his hair groomed with fragrant oil and neatly combed back. He sat on the edge of the chair, nervously clasping his hands together.

"Where is your parental house, barkhurdar?" asked Mian.

"Ji, my parents and family live in Lahore, and I am here on account of my job."

"Have you spoken to them about this match? Are they willing and happy with it?"

"Ji, I have spoken about it. They do have some reservations regarding the difference in our community, but I am sure they will come around once they meet you."

"I must also caution you that my daughters have been brought up in a free and progressive atmosphere. Sakina has a mind of her own and is not used to being coerced into following any restrictive traditions. I hope you will be able to respect that."

Ahmed nodded assent. "Ji, I understand."

Ahmed was seen off after being served with a lavish tea and snacks. Mian and Akhtar tactfully avoided any political discussions.

Mian Ali Beg paid a visit to Ahmed's parents in Lahore and finalized the marriage. Sakina was ecstatic and sent word to Nimmo, telling her to make sure to come and attend her wedding. She had felt rather lonely since Nimmo had left after her marriage, and was pining to meet her. Nimmo wrote to say that much as she wanted to come, her mother-in-law had refused permission because her sister-in-law Amaro was unwell, and Nimmo was expected to take care of the housework.

9

Memsahib

Cantonments were set up by the British as temporary en-campments for the military and their camp followers, and they slowly expanded to include Anglo-Indians, foreign businessmen, Eurasians and some 'privileged' native peo-ple. Each cantonment made available a segregated and safe place for military personnel, minimizing contact with the local civil population and creating a kind of regimented cultural pocket. The cantonment was designed to be self-sufficient and offered all facilities for European cultural and social needs. The Ambala army cantonment was set up in 1843 as a substitute for the cantonment in Karnal, which was hit by a malaria epidemic in 1841. It soon ac-quired the form of a district through the confiscation of 'jagir' territories of independent chieftains and those of Chaudhries and Lambardars of villages who had partici-pated in the rebellion of 1857. Many of them had been publicly hanged or deported to 'Kalapani'—the malaria-inflicted Andaman Islands. In 1858 the British established a penal colony at Port Blair for criminal convicts from the Indian subcontinent, including the infamous Cellular jail.

As Hukum Singh's jeep entered the city, he proudly pointed out to Nimmo the grand old white building of the Holy Redeemer's Church standing majestically on Lawrence road with a large brass bell hanging in its highest turret. Further down the road, they drove past the Imperial Bank of India and Capitol Cinema. A left turn led to a huge extended cemetery on Jagadhari road. The Gymkhana Club, with a well-trimmed garden, stood as a silent taunt to all who had no access to this elitist den of pleasure. As he pointed out the Garrison School for the children of military personnel, Nimmo imagined seeing her son here in some years. Broad, beautiful roads flanked with neat rows of Frangipani, Gulmohar and Amaltas trees ran through rows of whitewashed barracks and bungalows. Nimmo stared in awe at the sprawling hutments with high, red shingled roofs and acres of gardens around them, housing the white sahibs and their memsahibs. It was a long leap for her from the mud path of Sahnewal to the broad, straight and majestic 'Mall Road', with meticulously maintained belts of green grass and paved paths for pedestrians shaded by the 'Pride of India' trees. The Mall was swept clean by jemadars early in the morning, while Bhishtis with goat-skin bags slung over their shoulder, sprinkled down the dust with water. Nimmo strained her neck out to look at a white lady with a parasol, walking her dog on the Mall.

"Hai rabba, how white she is! Her legs are all naked!

Why is she carrying an umbrella when it's not even raining?"

"Don't stare; they are not like the Indian women. You will see more of them in the regiment," said Hukum Singh.

The end of the Mall led to the the Sadar Bazaar area where the entire cantonment population shopped. It catered to the high, fashionable taste of the Sahibs and their Memsahibs with a drapery store, shoe shop, crockery shop and other small shops for daily needs. Officers found it undignified to bargain or handle small cash, and it was customary for the shop-owner to note down the credit and send a bill at the end of the month. Private houses beyond the bazaar slowly thinned out to expansive cultivated fields.

British military authorities took their role of playing 'Mai-baap' to the soldiers very seriously indeed, right down to monitoring their sex life. The British soldier was not paid well enough to maintain a family and neither was he allowed to marry until he reached a certain rank. He could not possibly be expected to live a life of celibacy, and random philandering would result in incidences of venereal diseases. Therefore 'Lal Bazaars' (red-light districts) were allowed to function in all cantonments to satiate innate needs of the flesh. Brothels for sepoys and officers were strictly segregated and managed by madams, who were paid for their services from regimental funds. There were instances when the commanding officer of a regiment petitioned the local government officials to provide additional prostitutes for the troops to maintain a comfortable ratio! These brothels housed Indian women but were out of bounds for Indian men. Paradoxically, British officials were strictly discouraged from establishing any relationship with the native Indian women according to a policy formulated in late 1830. Nimmo was perplexed to see women with painted faces hanging out in the street as the jeep passed through the Lal Bazaar.

"Who are these women ji? Why are they all so painted up? Do they work in the Ram Leela?" she asked.

"They are kanjaris. You will find them at the outskirts of every cantonment. Since many men here are away from their families, it is a good market for them," said Hukum Singh.

"Oh! Do all faujis come to them?" asked Nimmo.

Hukum Singh looked away without replying.

Troops were accommodated in long brick barracks, while senior officers lived in opulent, large bungalows built in five to ten acres of land. The main house was generally built with high shingled roofs and surrounded with deep verandas on most sides to counter the heat. The kitchen was usually at some distance from the main house, connected to it through a covered pathway. The house was surrounded by well laid out gardens with a whole row of servant quarters near the back boundary wall. An officer's personal domestic staff included a khansamah, mali, dhobi, jemadar, driver and the children's ayah. Carriage house and stables had now given place to motor garages for the higher-ups while the junior officers rode bicycles. It was typical to find a set of cane chairs and table set out in the veranda, with hanging baskets holding green ferns. Thick mats called 'Tattis' woven from fragrant grass were hung in doorways and windows in the summer. These were drenched continuously with water so that breeze blowing through them would keep the house cool and sweet-smelling. Electric fans were slowly making their way into houses of senior officers, but many still had large fabric punkahs hung from beams in the roof. A long rope attached to the punkah led out of the window to be swung by young boys sitting out in the verandas to work up a breeze for the sahibs. They would tie one end of the rope to their toe, tugging at it till they dozed off from exhaustion and were yelled at to resume the exercise.

Nimmo was awed by this vast new world of parks, bazaars, cinema halls, clubs and grand buildings. Hukum Singh had been allotted a small bungalow in a cluster of similar ones for young officers, and in no time she set about cleaning and setting up her home. Huge brass pots and pans were displayed proudly on the kitchen shelves and beds covered with bedspreads she had brought in her trousseau, painstakingly embroidered in cross stitch by her and her mother over the years.

Everything was new and unfamiliar to Nimmo: the city people, challenges of running a new home and her role as an army wife. Most of the officers' wives in her neighbourhood were city-bred and sophisticated. They seemed to be smart and self-confident in their saris, sandals and makeup. Nimmo could not summon up the courage to approach them and kept to herself. She spent the day in the house, looking for something to do. Cooking a meal for two hardly took much time. Hukum Singh had admonished her when he found her cleaning the house, telling her it was below a memsahib's station. She couldn't get the hang of laying the table with forks and knives and preparing brewed tea in a pot, which was how Hukum Singh liked it. The bathroom flummoxed her. That it was attached right next to the bedroom seemed dirty. It had a huge cast iron tub which she used for washing clothes till Hukum Singh told her it was meant to sit in and bathe. He liked to indulge himself in the tub on Sundays, directing his batman to prepare the gusul. Nimmo couldn't imagine soaking in a pool of one's scum. She was utterly repelled by the thunder-boxes or commodes placed in the bathroom for one's morning business and was most uncomfortable for the first few days. A commode consisted of a removable tin receptacle placed in a hollow cutout in the centre of a wooden chair. All bathrooms had a backdoor for giving access to the scavenger, who removed the pots and replaced them after cleaning them out. There was a porcelain sink in the corner for washing hands and brushing one's teeth. Nimmo was happy to use a toothbrush instead of a Neem twig, enjoying the fresh aroma of the toothpaste.

The lady next door came over to visit her one evening.

"I am Mrs Pritam. You are new here; please let me know if there is anything I can do for you."

"Sat Sri Akal behen ji. Where are you from?" asked Nimmo.

"We are from Jammu. And you?"

"We are Jat Sikhs from near Ludhiana, ji. Which village are your parents from, and what may be your caste ji?" asked Nimmo.

"We are Dogras. My parents are from Srinagar."

"Are men from different castes working together here?"

"The army is beyond religion and caste," explained

Mrs. Pritam with a smile. "All men work together here. There may be a caste-based biradari in villages, but here there is a biradari based on your regiment. All those who pick up arms to serve in the regiment become brothers in a way because they will fight to save each other's lives if the need arises."

"Hindu, Musalman, Isai and Sikhs all eat together?" asked Nimmo incredulously.

"Yes, certainly."

"I wish that was so everywhere," said Nimmo.

Hukum Singh donned his sports kit and left for the morning parade before sunrise on sounding of the Reveille bugle. He returned home for breakfast and a bath, donning his olive-green uniform to proceed for office, education classes or weapon training as per schedule. The orderly took care of Hukum Singh's clothes and accessories, shining his shoes and brass epaulettes till you could see your face in them. He returned home for lunch, followed by an afternoon siesta after which he again left for games. He played hockey, one of the more popular games with Punjabis. The Retreat bugle would sound at sunset when everyone was expected to drop whatever they were doing to stand in attention in memory of lost soldiers. The flag on the unit quarter guard was lowered at this time, and there was a change of guard with the night guards taking their posts.

Evenings were for visits to the club or the mess for a game of cards or mahjong, but Nimmo could not gather enough courage to go. She struggled to cope up with empty hours that stretched out into lonely evenings. She would sit and look out of the window for Hukum Singh to return from office and her heart still missed a beat when she caught sight of him entering the gate. Days passed, but Hukum Singh stayed cold and distant. He was reluctant to take her out with him and seldom invited anyone home. Nimmo started losing confidence and withdrew further into her shell. Her old identity was gone. She was no longer the bubbly, carefree Nimmo who played with five pebbles and was proud of her embroidery and weaving skills. She could not fit into her new persona of a memsahib. It was a mismatch. She would be startled when the orderly addressed her as 'memsahib'. Was that her?

"Try to learn the ways of the city now that you have come here," said Hukum Singh. "The city is very different from the village; people live differently here, dress differently. Get ready to go to the welfare centre tomorrow. CO Sahib's memsahib will be meeting with the officers' wives."

"No ji, let me stay at home. I won't go. I know nothing about what to say or do there."

"Don't be such an ignorant clod. I wish I could hide you away somewhere to avoid the embarrassment you cause me. But it is expected that you present yourself to CO Sahib's memsahib, and it can't be avoided. All other officers' wives will be going too. You can go along with Lt. Nek Chand's wife next-door. Dress up decently."

Next day, Nimmo timidly went up to knock on her neighbour's door. Lt. Nek Chand's wife peered out of her door and looked her up and down, suppressing an amused smile. Nimmo stood decked in a new salwar suit from her trousseau, hanging loosely on her spare frame and her veil drawn low over her forehead. She wore a gold necklace set around her neck, her face heavily coated with Afghan

Snow cream and a smatter of lipstick on her lips.

"Behen ji, will you please take me along to the Welfare Centre?"

"Of course. Please come in. You look so pretty." She said with effortless hypocrisy which comes so naturally to women paying false compliments.

The meeting at the Welfare Centre was a daunting experience for Nimmo. She could not stop ogling at the 'bara memsahib' who was so fair with golden hair and blue eyes. She wore a sleeveless pink frock and high heels. How did she manage to balance herself on them? Mrs Gillespie tried to speak to her kindly, but not much communication could happen with her inadequate Hindustani and Nimmo's rustic Punjabi.

"Welcome to the Center. Sab theek hai?" asked Mrs Gillespie.

"Hanji," Nimmo's voice seemed to choke in her throat.

"Koi pareshani to nahi?"

"Hanji," said Nimmo.

"Is there anything you need? Kuch mangta?"

"Hanji," was all that Nimmo could respond with. There were muffled sniggers around her.

Women shared embroidery patterns and chocolate fondue recipes, chatting animatedly among themselves during the high tea served later. Nimmo spent most of the time huddled in a corner, mortified to see women look at her with snide whispers and smiles. She came home and cried to herself. They all seemed to belong here; smart, confident and capable. She could speak neither English nor Hindi and felt lost. Why were they snickering at her? How would she ever fit in?

Hukum Singh returned for lunch to find her downcast and puffy-eyed.

"How did it go? Did you wish Mrs Gillespie?"

"I was so nervous and confused ji. I couldn't think of what to say. What kind of women are the mems? Their skin is so white...and what strange cat eyes ji! Her hair is so golden! Are they all like that in vilayat? Hai, she was wearing just a short frock with her legs all naked! And she wore red sandals with such high heels; I was afraid she might fall any time."

"This is how British women dress. They are educated and smart, unlike most backward Indian women. I was told that you have primary education, but apparently, it was a lie. You can't even make simple conversation. I wonder what she must be thinking about my marrying an uneducated woman! You are not in the village any longer and must learn English and how to move around in society."

A tutor was engaged to teach Nimmo English. However much she tried, she could not get the hang of the language. Her Punjabi tongue continued to pronounce 'family' as 'phamily' and 'please' as 'pleej'. She felt like a failure and started avoiding her classes. There was considerable social activity in the unit, and Hukum Singh tried to persuade Nimmo to attend some events where wives were invited. How was she to understand the git-mit of the officers' wives around her? She would undoubtedly trip and fall if she tried to wrap herself in six yards of a sari and try and walk on high heels! There seemed to be unending events of garden parties, polo matches, horse shows and dinner dances at the Army Club. Whenever she made an effort to go out with Hukum Singh, he came home and ridiculed her for some social error or omission. She became increasingly nervous, committing more faux pax as she lost confidence.

One evening Hukum Singh invited two of his friends and their wives home for drinks. Having been pulled up by her brother-in-law for facing strangers with a naked face, Nimmo walked in with her veil drawn low on her face. She mumbled a reply to their greetings and sat on the furthest chair in the drawing-room while the bearer served drinks and snacks. Their conversation soon turned to the unrest regarding independence, something which was being discussed all over.

"The situation seems to be going from bad to worse," said Captain Sadiq. "Have you heard, the Deputy Commissioners have been instructed to prepare a list of all Congress party members who will be arrested if the Congress votes for Gandhi's Civil Disobedience Resolution?"

"Yes, it could be a very tricky situation, and the army may be called in to help the civil administration," said Hukum Singh. "Two years ago, before either of you was posted here, we were called in to tackle a group of armed revolutionaries who attacked the Mission Compound and the Police Station, killing six Britishers and grabbing some arms and ammunition. We moved in and rounded them up in no time, shooting down eight of them and capturing six who were hanged to death later. For four days the district was literally handed over to the control of the Brigade Commander. Indians are fools if they think they can get the better of the British might."

"Don't you think two hundred years of exploitation of our country is a long enough time?" said Captain Rathore.

"The world wars have sapped their resources and Britain is no longer the power that it was. They are barely able to find enough money to feed their armies and civil authorities. They have had to give in to the Congress and other national organizations and remit the sentences of three senior officers of the Indian National Army. Believe me, their days in Hindustan are numbered now."

"If the British leave, who will operate the Railways, banks, posts and telegraphs, depots and factories, hospitals and other civil services? I think this entire system will collapse, and there will be total chaos with the Hindus and Muslims flying at each other's throats," said Mrs Sadiq.

"One must not forget the humiliation they have put Indians through," said Captain Rathore. "Till very recently, the British officers were extremely uncomfortable about Indian officers joining the Gymkhana Club. Even Indian officers of the elite Civil Services were not admitted as guests, let alone as members. But then came the World War and the British government was in dire need of men to fight. Indian officers were recruited in huge numbers against short service commission. Army Stations began to overflow with a large number of King's Indian Commissioned Officers. By law, they could not refuse membership to those who were Commissioned Indian officers of the King-Emperor, as any member who was in the station automatically became a member and had to pay his subscription whether he used the club facilities or not. The snooty white club administration tried to find subtle ways of keeping the native officers out, tweaking rules to increase club subscriptions so much that they could hardly afford to visit the club at all. They were forbidden to bring any

Anglo-Indian or Indian guests to the club. The British members made the Indian officers feel so uncomfortable and unwelcome that none summoned the courage to use the pool, enter the bar or dine, with most of them limiting themselves to a game at the Tennis court, after which they returned to their quarters."

"That does sound unfair, but things have changed since then. Do you think anyone can really take their place? What do you say, Nimmo ji?" asked Mrs Sadiq, trying to include her in the conversation.

Nimmo wanted to remind them of the 1919 carnage by General Dyer in Amritsar and the great efforts and sacrifices being made by the 'Gadhari Babas' and the armed revolutionary groups inspired by the sacrifices of Bhagat Singh, Kartar Singh Sarabha and Rajguru. She wanted to tell them to step out of their slavish mentality to the British and think about their country, but she was tongue-tied due to her lack of confidence and could not speak. She just nodded and managed to say,

"I don't know much about politics ji."

Hukum Singh accosted her soon after his friends left.

"What kind of a village fool have I landed up with? I was so embarrassed in front of my friends. You have no grooming at all. Why did you come in with a veil drawn over your face? Go and look in the mirror. Do you think you are some hoori the likes of which no one has seen before? Were my friends going to gobble you up? Can't you learn to dress properly? Did you see their smart wives? Bringing you here with me was a big mistake; I should have left you behind in the village itself."

Nimmo had never felt so inadequate, so humiliated in

her life. Her face flushed crimson with shame. She had held herself superior to other girls in her village, being the Zaildar's daughter and generally adept at most household chores girls her age were supposed to know. She was proud of her ability to read and write Punjabi and do basic math, skills not common to most girls then. Her family and her aunts had all said that she was a clever girl. What was the use of it all if it did not make her good enough for her husband? Her lack of urban sophistication was hardly her fault. How could she be what she was not? He did lift the mosquito net over her bed every night, slipping in beside her for as long as he needed her, after which he would roll over and leave for his bed. It never occurred to her to refuse him. Howsoever disdainful his behaviour towards her; he was still her husband. She felt a lesser person for being rejected and cried herself to a troubled sleep. She dreamed of being thirteen again and playing hide and seek with Sakina, Shammi, Bholan, Waseem and Akhtar. She had hidden behind the bush in the courtyard when Akhtar came and tapped her on the shoulder.

"There you are! I will eventually find you wherever you may hide!" he laughed.

10

Looking Back

Hukum Singh was promoted and sent to Peshawar in the North-West Frontier Provinces, where Pathan tribals kept up unrelenting guerrilla warfare against the British armies. It was one of the most fought after frontiers ever, with fierce Afghan mountain tribes raiding and plundering the North-Indian plains at their will. Peshawar division, including Attock, Rawalpindi, Jhelum and Murree, was the largest and the most important in India.

The cantonment in Peshawar had been planned in a very restricted area to make it easily defensible against raids of Afridis and other hostile tribes from the neighbouring mountains, which constantly descended into the plains for plunder. But the overcrowding in the tropical Indian climate created very unhealthy conditions for the troops, making Peshawar a dreaded place of posting.

Hukum Singh wrote home to say that the provisions for water supply and sanitation were very poor, making them vulnerable to tropical diseases like malaria and dysentery. Each house had to have a chowkidar from the local tribals, which was an understood arrangement to keep one's horse and belongings safe. Such was the ever-present danger from the tribals that no one was allowed to venture beyond the line of sentries once the sun had set, and even in daylight, never too far from the station. There were frequent thefts and many a times young sepoys had to face harsh trials for their carelessness. Hukum Singh recounted a most distressing episode of a flogging parade, in which fifty lashes were given as punishment to two young Artillerymen for losing their kits. They were stripped to the waist and flogged publicly for their offences. Hukum Singh was part of many ongoing skirmishes with the Afridis and other Afghan tribes, and his family worried for him and prayed for his safe return.

Nimmo took this opportunity to go to her parents' house in Sahnewal. Spring ushered in mellow, balmy days imbued with heady fragrances of blooming flowers and ripening crops. Expansive acres of wheat fields were touched with an exuberant golden hue. Falling on the fifth day of the Indian calendar month of Magh, Basant announced the end of winter and ushered in spring. Though Hindus celebrated it by worshipping Goddess Saraswati, few villagers had any inkling about it, and celebrated it as a seasonal festival. Women bathed early and wore yellow dupattas to go to the gurudwara and pay obeisance on the festival of Basant Panchami. Chinti cooked yellow saffron halwa to take as an offering. They sat and listened to Bhai ji read out the 'Basant ki Vaar' along with other worship-pers, both Sikh and Hindu.

A gentle, mellifluous breeze blew over the rooftops, and bright multi-coloured kites bobbed up and down against a crystal blue sky. Returning from school, boys hurriedly threw aside their school bags and rushed to the roof to fly their newly-bought, multi-coloured kites. Anxious mothers worried about their overstepping the roof edge, warning them to be careful. There were fierce competitions for grabbing each other's kites. Whenever someone captured a kite, the place would reverberate with triumphant shouts of 'Bo-kata'!

The clock seemed to have turned back for Nimmo, and she felt carefree and rejuvenated in her parental home. Sakina had married and gone to her in-laws house in Malerkotla. But Nimmo was happy to be back with her mother and sister Bholan, who had metamorphosed from a gangly teenager to a pretty young girl and spent more time in the kitchen now than playing geete and stapu. Maji was getting weaker with age but continued to wield authority in the house. Nama Taya's condition seemed to have worsened, and he was often violent and abusive. It disturbed Nimmo that he was terrified of the Zaildar and would start whimpering and hiding whenever he saw him.

Nimmo felt a stronger bond with her mother now that she was herself a married woman and they lay down to-gether many a night, sharing their concerns and worries till the little earthenware lamp flickered and died out. They talked about Nimmo's life in the cantonment, the white mems and sahibs. They bitched about her mother-in-law and Amaro. Chinti filled her in with details about all that had happened in the village while she had been away. Her friends Baggi and Tippi had been married off. Baggi had found a good match in a nearby village, but Tippi had been married off to a much older man in Doaba as a second wife. The Daroga's wife had finally had a son after four daughters. There had been a recent dacoity in the Majri, and now every village observed a vigil at night. She was dying to know if Akhtar was married yet or not, but dared not ask her mother directly.

"How is Hajjo massi and Shammi?"

"They are all very well. Sakina is happy with her husband and they are on the lookout for a good match for Shammi. The boys are totally immersed in political jalse and all. Hajjo worries a lot about their safety. Your father keeps reassuring them that no one can touch a hair on their heads till we are alive. May Waheguru keep peace in the country."

In spite of their closeness, there were many things which Nimmo could not bring herself to tell Chinti. She did not tell her about Hukum Singh's cold attitude towards her, nor how she felt small and a total misfit in his circle, how she never seemed to measure up to his expectations. She also did not tell her that she knew that he flirted with an Anglo-Indian nurse in the Army hospital. It would make her mother worry and underline her failure as a wife, for she remembered the derision her Bhua faced for failing to please her husband. Sympathy was the last thing that girls could expect when complaining against their husbands. Women were wired to keep silent and accept whatever fate handed out to them.

Bholan was very curious about her life in Ambala.

"Behen, have you sat in a green fauji motor? How fast does it go? Do you feel scared? Does Jeeja ji carry a big gun like the ones they show in the film? Behen, what are the mems like? I heard they smoke cigarettes like men? Is it true? What is your bungalow like? Please take me with you when you go back?"

"Look at her going on! Find her a fauji boy too, Nimmo. She is so fascinated by the fauj," said Chinti.

"Oh no," reverted Nimmo vehemently. "Not at all. You must find her a good simple zamindar boy nearby. Some things look good only from afar."

Chinti and Bholan looked at her in surprise, but she got up and left before they could ask further questions.

One afternoon Jamalo walked in looking for Nimmo.

"Biba ji, I have brought you some news that will make you very happy. Your friend Sakina has just arrived from her in-laws' village. The first thing she asked on getting down from the tonga was—Jamalo, what is the news about Nimmo? She jumped for joy to hear that you are here and has sent me running to call you to meet her."

Nimmo grabbed her dupatta and rushed next door to Sakina's house. Both friends hugged each other and cried and laughed together, overcome by strong emotions. Nimmo noticed that Sakina was pregnant. She seemed to glow with health and wellbeing.

"I see that I am going to become a massi soon. How many months gone are you?" she asked.

"Seven months. And when are you going to return the favour?" asked Sakina.

"Have you brought along my Jeeja or come alone?" Nimmo asked, changing the topic.

"He will come to fetch me back, and you can meet him then," she laughed.

Nimmo's eyes searched for Akhtar as both of them went inside to sit and chat.

"So how is your husband? What are your in-laws like? I hope your mother-in-law doesn't make much trouble for you?" asked Nimmo.

"A mother-in-law would not be true to her kind if she did not make trouble for her daughter-in-law!" laughed Sakina. "But I just disregard it all because Ahmed takes care of me. His love makes me forget all that his mother or sister may do or say to trouble me."

"You are truly a lucky woman, Sakina," Nimmo said with a touch of wistfulness.

"Look at you, a memsahib living in a bungalow in a city! We are just simple village folk leading ordinary lives. Tell me about your life. It must be so exciting for you to move around in the cantonment with its mall roads and gardens! You must be meeting and mixing with white mems and sahibs. How big is your bungalow? But why are you looking weak? Are you eating angrezi food now?" Sakina asked many questions in a row.

After a long time, Nimmo felt she could finally confide in someone. She poured her heart out to Sakina.

"I could not become a memsahib, and I have not been able to fit in the world of bungalows. I don't very often meet with the mems, except the CO Sahib's wife in the welfare centre. I know no English and feel very foolish and ignorant meeting with other wives. He is not very keen to take me out because most of his officer friends have educated wives from cities who look down upon me. I can do nothing right and am an embarrassment to him. He does not miss a chance to humiliate me and looks down on me as an uncouth villager. Most of his time is spent outside the house, and I know he is carrying on with an Anglo-Indian nurse from the Army hospital. I feel extremely lonely and dejected. Though I worry for his well being after his posting in Peshawar, it is a Godsend opportunity for me to come back home and spend time with my family.

"Hai Allah! This is terrible! And I have been thinking that you are fate's favoured one! Who can foresee a girl's future after marriage? It is like a second birth for us. Let's hope that things will be better once you have a child."

"I don't know. There are no signs of a child yet. His family resents me for not having conceived."

Sakina's mother came in and hugged Nimmo affectionately.

"Daughter Nimmo, have you become so busy with your husband and in-laws that you do not pay your village a visit for so long? You seem to have forgotten us all after going to the city."

Nimmo returned her hug affectionately.

"No massi, nothing can ever make me forget you and your love. How much control does a married woman have over her own life? You have to ask for permission for everything."

"Ammi, I don't see Akhtar and Waseem anywhere. Where are they off to?" asked Sakina.

"What should I tell you, daughter. They are both involved with God knows what jalse and meetings and are away most of the time, sometimes for days. I worry a lot for their safety. Muslims are being targeted in many places and people say the country will be split into two. Many Muslim families have started moving to lehnda Punjab."said Hajjo.

"Massi, how can anyone even think of leaving behind their ancestral homes and land and moving to another place?" replied Nimmo. "I am sure no one can ever divide our country. This mad violence between Hindu and Muslims that has been fanned by some leaders will soon die down and things will be normal again."

"You are right, daughter. All my ancestors were born and died on this very land. My body is made from the elements of this soil and it will be buried here when I die. No one can push us out from our own home and land. May Allah bring dozakh to the people who are clamouring, to separate brother from brother and split this land." said Hajjo.

"Inshah Allah, Ammi," said Sakina. "But Ahmed is very worried about the escalating incidences of violence in the cities. The recent massive riots in Calcutta have posed a question mark over the future of Muslims in India and triggered an unstoppable spiral of communal violence across the country. Do you know that the Hindu-Muslim riots there have left over ten thousand people dead and many more wounded? It seems that Muslims are no longer welcome in their own country. The Home Rule Bill was passed in 1935 and the first provincial governments formed in 1937. In the United provinces, Congress rejected the Muslim League's offer to form a coalition government, insisting that they merge in Congress to get a share in governance. The separate electorates system did not fare well for Muslims all over the country. This caused much heart-burning in the Muslims and Jinnah's Muslim League raised a demand for the separate state of Pakistan in 1940."

They were still chatting when Akhtar walked in, followed by Waseem. The unexpectedness of seeing Nimmo stopped him in his tracks. He couldn't take his eyes off her face. Here she sat in his house, a deep blue dupatta flung across her shoulders, half trailing on the floor as always. It was as if she had never gone away. As she turned around to face him, he saw she was thinner, making her face more angular and mystical. Her eyes seemed larger in her thinner face and somehow very forlorn. A bunch of stray hair fell across her forehead, and a nose pin shone on the side of her nose. Nimmo was transfixed seeing him stand before her in the same white kurta pyjama and jacket that he usually wore. How often she had wondered what he would look like now. How long she had waited to see him again. She noticed the changes that age and maturity bring; he seemed more filled out, self-assured and staid. His bronze complexion was more tanned and he had grown a beard. She was still gazing at him when his face broke out into a large smile.

"So you have found your way back to our humble village, Memsahib. We thought you had forgotten all about us in your new world of sahibs and bungalows. How is your Captain Mian?" he asked.

Nimmo did not much want to talk about Hukum Singh. He did not seem to belong to this part of her world.

"He is posted in Peshawar right now."

"Please suggest a good girl for him, Nimmo," complained Sakina. "He has been so busy fighting for national issues that he refuses to think about his marriage. Whether Pakistan is made or not is another story, but his home and hearth will certainly never be made if he keeps putting it off any longer. Tell me who will marry an old, middle-aged man? All the best girls are already taken."

Nimmo turned to look at him questioningly. "So what kind of girl is janaab looking for?"

"I promise that I will agree to marry any girl that Nimmo selects for me. But she must make sure that the girl is worthy of me in every way," laughed Akhtar.

Nimmo held his gaze for a moment and saw a reflection of the tenderness they had once shared. A secret joy and exhilaration shot through her mind and body. She blushed and lowered her eyes.

"That is a very difficult responsibility, indeed, because only the best of girls will be worthy of you. But I will certainly try and find this girl from wherever she has been hiding for so long," she replied lightly.

"So tell us the latest updates about the freedom movement Bhai jaan? Do you think the country will be ultimately divided?" asked Sakina.

"We are hoping and praying that the leaders see sense and this calamity can be stopped. But many Muslims fear being dominated by the Hindu majority Congress, and demand a separate nation as suggested by Jinnah. The massive riots at Calcutta have added to the insecurity of Muslims. A similar demand, of course, was first made in 1906 by Agha Khan, who led a delegation to meet the Viceroy on behalf of the Muslims. Though Jinnah did not advocate a separate sovereign state till 1940, he has started to feel more and more marginalized by the Congress. But all who support a two-nation theory fail to realize that it is a dirty trick of the British to try and fragment our country before they leave. They have achieved creating a fissure between the communities by placing us on a separate electorate."

Waseem, who had been listening, joined in.

"The Hindu revivalists are worsening the situation by trying to give the nation a Hindu character by demanding a ban on cow slaughter and adoption of 'Bande-matram' as the national song, which is linked to anti-Muslim sentiment. The Muslim League, Akali Dal and the Hindu Mahasabha have rejected the pluralist paradigm, which has been the bedrock of a united India. The religious fundamentalists are baying for a Hindu state or an Islamic theocracy."

"We at the Azad Muslim Conference, along with the Khaksars, will fight to keep our country united, Inshah Allah! Gandhi is not in favour of partition either." Akhtar's face came to glow as he spoke, showing his deep faith and commitment to his chosen cause.

Nimmo was visibly moved by his speech. She felt helpless that she could not be actively involved in the struggle for freedom and admired Sakina and Shammi for being more active. Akhtar was surprised when Nimmo took off the pair of gold bangles she was wearing and handed them to him.

"This is my humble contribution to your efforts," she said.

"I certainly cannot accept these, please keep them," said Akhtar.

"I cannot physically join in our freedom movement in any way, so please let me not carry the guilt of having made no contribution at all. How will I live with it?" she asked.

Akhtar reached out to take the bangles and their hands touched for a while too long. The gramophone on the corner table of the baithak played a popular song in Begum Akhtar's plaintive voice 'Koyaleeya mat kar pukaar, karejva mein laage kataar' (Do not call through your song, koel; it pierces my heart like a dagger). It reminded her of days gone past, bringing back the flavour of evenings spent in the warmth of this home and family; of the intense poignancy of a relationship which could never quite find its culmination; of thwarted aspirations and unrequited emotions. She looked up at Akhtar and held his gaze for a moment before getting up to return to her mother's home. She could read the same pain and longing reflected in his eyes too.

11

Cicadas in the Night

The wheat crop had been harvested and stored, and the vast, open fields with stubble stood empty and forlorn. A few laggards threshed the wheat spikes against a horizontally laid drum, causing a lot of chaff to blow around in the air, covering everything with a layer of dust. High velocity dust storms often caused spooky whirlwinds, called 'ghost winds', to whiz across the fields. Heat waves drove everyone to stay indoors most for of the day except early mornings and evenings. People consumed large amounts of churned lassi and sattu to keep themselves cool.

Nimmo had not heard from Hukum Singh. She consoled herself that he was posted at a remote station, and it was not easy to send letters from there. She was happy to spend time with Bholan, Sakina, Shammi and relive her childhood memories. Sakina lent her some books by Amrita Pritam and Dhani Ram Chatrik, which opened a new world to her. She found her old confidence in herself returning. She also got to see Akhtar off and on, and found herself looking forward to her visits to Sakina's house. It was fascinating to hear his accounts about the freedom struggle, and she developed a great admiration for his efforts.

Chinti was worried that Nimmo had not yet conceived after two years of marriage. She had offered ardas and karah parshad at the gurudwara and made mannats for offering a degh of zarda at the peer's dargah. Hukum Singh was a big officer, and there would be no dearth of girls available to him for a second marriage. No one would find fault with his parents if they chose to get him remarried. Who would tolerate a barren wife?

She had heard of a much-acclaimed sadhu in Rishikesh who was blessed with the power to bestow children to barren women.

Amavas was the dark, moonless night potent with possibilities when spirits used their powers to culminate the desires of those who could please them. It was a night of magical outcomes and changing of destinies. Chinti set off for Rishikesh with Nimmo on amavas to fulfill a mannat she had made with Ganga mai and visit the sadhu.

It was an exciting journey for Nimmo who had not had many chances to travel. The bus sped over potholed roads to enter the foothills, and she gazed curiously out of the bus window at the changing scenery. They crossed small villages with thatched huts where women in saris stopped to gape at the bus. Men working in the field wore small dhotis which looked more like loincloths. Rangy, dappled cows lazily grazed in the open lands. The last leg of the journey took the bus through lush forest areas of the

Himalayan foothills, allowing only filtered rays of sunlight to pass through.

"Bebe, are there tigers in this jungle?" asked Nimmo.

"Yes there are but don't worry, they don't come out in the day time," replied Chinti.

They reached the Rishikesh ashram late in the evening and were shown to a room furnished with bare necessities. Nimmo opened the window to look at the mighty, untamed Ganges flowing past, it's dark, swirling waters rumbling and crashing against the banks, making a constant roaring sound. A group of bearded sadhus in loin cloths, matt-haired and smeared with ash, sang the evening aarti on the river bank, holding lighted lamps in their hands. The lamps spread a dim yellow glow around them, giving a surreal look to the place. Many pilgrims and devotees sang along devotedly to the tinkle of brass bells, carrying a hundred desperate longings in their hearts. It was a pretty and serene picture.

"I came here with other women of the family to bathe in the holy Ganga ten years back. My brother was ill with a mysterious fever which refused to go away. We went to every vaid and hakim we were told of, but the fever refused to go. Then we brought him to Ganga mai. One dip in the river and the fever started going down the next day. I am sure Ganga mai will fill your lap too. The Swami Ji who heads this ashram has blessed many infertile women with children."

Chinti and Nimmo went down to the Ganga ghat for a dip. The water was cold and took away Nimmo's breath for a moment. But she felt energized and renewed after the holy bath; maybe Ganga mai had washed away the curse on her destiny, she thought. They were summoned for Swami Ji's darshan after dinner. A fair, middle-aged well-built man with a bare shaven head reclined against a long cushion on a mattress placed on the floor. He wore an orange kurta and dhoti, a rudraksha mala around his neck and gold hoop earrings in his ears. His forehead bore the U-mark of Vishnu in sandalwood paste. His muscular legs were half bare in his short dhoti. He appraised them with a benign smile on his face. Jeeti and Nimmo bowed to him and sat cross-legged in front of him.

"I can see that you are plagued with problems, devi," he turned to speak to Nimmo. "You can open your heart to me. Tell me what is troubling you. Does your husband neglect you? And you have not been blessed with a Bal Gopal yet?"

Chinti immediately bowed down to his feet. "You are truly a realized soul. You have guessed our problem correctly. My daughter has not conceived after having been married for more than two years and I am afraid that her husband will take a second wife. We have come to you with great hope. Please bless her with a son."

Swami Ji calculated an auspicious time for a special puja and asked Nimmo to come to his room exactly at midnight. Both mother and daughter stayed awake lest they miss the given time. Nimmo entered Swami Ji's room at the given hour. He sat with his eyes closed, mumbling something. He opened his eyes for a moment and gestured for her to sit. Smoke arose from some ambers in an iron skillet in front of him. He threw some powder in it which let out an acrid smell. It made her feel light-headed.

"Devi, come here and let me cleanse you of your curse

of infertility." He rose and reached out to Nimmo, running his hands all over her groping her breasts. "Remove your clothes," he said, lifting her shirt and tugging at her salwar drawstring.

"What...what are you doing, Swami Ji," stuttered Nimmo, feeling a little disoriented. The smoke seemed to be inebriating her.

"I am giving you what you want, girl. You want a son. I will give you one. Don't you know how sons are conceived?" he sneered.

Shocked and repulsed, Nimmo struggled to push him away and ran out of the room. She sobbed and told her mother about the incident. She was in for a second shock.

"You fool, can you not understand that you must give your husband a child if you are to stay in that house?" said Jeeti. "Any means to beget that child are justified for securing your future. For centuries women have known that many times the fault lies not with the woman, but the man. But who will ever admit it and insult his manhood? Women's chastity is a small sacrifice to uphold their husband's ego and secure their future. This is the one way out that women have used secretly to beget children. No one is any wiser, and everyone is happy. I thought you were old enough to understand this without me spelling it out for you. Not just common women, even desperate queens have resorted to this trick to beget heirs to thrones."

"Hai, hai, Bebe, I cannot imagine women have been sleeping with strangers to beget a child. How does it make them different from cows and buffaloes? I will not do it. I cannot prostitute myself and let the seed of a stranger grow in me. Let's leave first thing in the morning. God will take care of my destiny."

The women returned home with no one being wiser about the whole mission. Nimmo spent many anxious moments wondering if Bebe's fears were correct and Hukum Singh might take a second wife. She had failed to come up to his expectations, nor had she borne him a child. Having rejected her mother's suggestion of begetting a child with a stranger, she could not help but think that if what Bebe said was indeed true, and the fault lay with Hukum, why could she not have a child with Akhtar? She blushed at her brazenness and pushed the thought away.

Some days later, she sat embroidering a bedsheet in the inner courtyard when Satta, the rathwan from her in-laws' house, called out from the main entrance.

"Sat Sri Akal Zaildar Sahib! Are you well and healthy? I have been sent to fetch Biba ji. Please get her ready to leave."

Satta was served a sumptuous meal and gifted a hand-woven khes, as Nimmo packed her clothes.

"Bhai, has no one from the family come with you to fetch her? Is Kaka ji back from Peshawar or not?" asked the Zaildar.

"Kaptaan sahib is back from Peshawar by Guru's grace. Rano's wedding has been decided for the coming pooranmasi, and everyone is busy with preparations. I have been asked to invite you all for the wedding."

The Zaildar fumed at this veiled insult to his daughter and family. Hukum Singh should have come himself to fetch Nimmo and extend the invitation for his sister's marriage. If not, someone else from the family should have made an effort. Anyhow, a daughter's parents must always show restraint. It would not do to show anger, especially when the girl was childless. A wedded girl belonged with her husband. Nimmo was seen off with customary gifts of ghee and sweets.

***

Hukum Singh's parents had started doubting Nimmo's ability to bear children. Two years was a long time for a woman to go without conceiving. Nobody could be happy just looking at a woman's face. Where was the solace in being such a big officer if there was no pitter-patter of little children running around in the house? Look at his bad stars—tied down with an infertile woman who enjoyed all the advantages of being a memsahib without giving him any heirs! Jeeti and Bhua may not have agreed on everything in the domestic power arena, but gladly joined forces for a common adversary—the younger daughter-in-law. Women nurtured an inherent desire to see their father's name carried forward through their brother's progeny, and Bhua was equally disappointed that Nimmo had failed to give her brother a grandson.

When Nimmo left for her parents' house, Bhua suggested visiting a Pandit in Ludhiana, who was highly accomplished in astrology and known to offer effective remedies for various problems. Pandit Rewa Das listened to their woes as a doctor listens to a patient's symptoms. The potbellied, bespectacled Pandit went through a prolonged exercise of consulting old, dusty books, drew up a horoscope and finally gave his prescription.

"You did well in approaching me. Mangal is favourable

to you this week. I have a solution that will solve both your problems. Your daughter-in-law is accursed and incapable of bearing children. You will have to remarry your son if you want any heirs from him. I can suggest a most suitable girl for him who will bring prosperity and grandsons to your house; a real Lakshmi. It will also solve the problem of your daughter's marriage. But remember, you have only one week to take action before Mangal changes its house again."

After a long consultation with the Pandit and a hefty offering, Jeeti and Bhua returned home with a new spring in their steps.

The very next day, Jeeti donned her best blue ghagra with a pink border and chikan-work chadar and summoned the rath to take her to her parental village. Bhua accompanied her in a more toned-down ensemble of a black soof ghagra and green silk chadar with purple threadwork stripes. Jeeti wanted no one to get a whiff of her plan, so it would not do to involve the local nai. She decided to send the nai of her parental village to Nabha carrying gifts—five seers of pinnis with flaxseed and almonds, and two seers of bhugga, a winter delicacy made with sesame seeds and condensed milk. No one knew what their mission was, and they offered no details. The rath ambled back into the outer courtyard of the haveli in the evening, and Jeeti entered the house to hug Rano with a sparkle in her eyes.

"Girls, get the baithak ready, there are guests arriving tomorrow. They will have lunch here. I want no compromise in hospitality. Start preparing now. Kala, go and ask the halwai for fresh jalebis and gulab jamuns. Rano and

Veero, both of you come in here and listen to me now. Amaro, see that the courtyard is swept clean. I don't want stinking dung heaps around. Get out the new china tea set and have it cleaned."

Sardar Naib Singh returned from his sojourn to find the house in a frenzy of activity. He gave his wife a questioning look; she drew him aside to update him about their meeting with the Pandit and his proposal.

"I hope you know what you are doing. Is the boy unmarried?"

"Yes, he is. And it is a well-to-do family with thirty acres of irrigated land. Do you think such a respected Pandit would suggest someone unworthy?"

"And he is healthy and not an addict?"

"I don't know how many more questions will you ask. Please pray to Waheguru that everything works out well."

"I just want to know whether they have asked all the questions about your daughter. If tomorrow those women spurn her and go back, how big an insult will it be for us? The whole village will mock us. And what about the Zaildar? He is not going to be happy about this."

Jeeti gave him a hard, cold look to dissuade any further discussion.

"The Zaildar could not produce a son in his home, and his daughter cannot produce even a lamb. Are we to blame for it? Should I sacrifice my son's welfare because of a barren woman? Don't worry. Everything will be fine. I have promised an offering at the gurudwara and the mazar of Sai Peer."

***

Nimmo sensed a chill in the air when she returned to Raikot. She hugged and congratulated Jeeti and Amaro for Rano's wedding, but they avoided meeting her gaze. Rano was in a state of elation and gave her a big hug. Bau ji met Nimmo with melancholy in his eyes as he placed his old gnarled hands on her head to bless her.

"May Waheguru bless you, daughter. Who can anticipate His games? Live long. May you remain a suhagan always."

There were only a few days to go for the wedding and preparations were in full swing. The cook had arrived and set up his kitchen in the backyard, his huge iron skillet letting out swirling mists of steam from cooking sweets, wafting mouthwatering aromas around the entire house. Nimmo found that all other women had received new clothes for the wedding except her. Hurt and angry, she confronted Jeeti.

"Bebe ji, did you forget all about me when you bought clothes for yourself and others? How will it look if the daughter-in-law of the house attends the wedding in old clothes?"

"Don't make a needless fuss and climb on my head. Are people coming to look at you hoorpari? It's not like new clothes are going to make you look any better. You can wear clothes from your trousseau. As if we don't have enough expenses already," said Jeeti, averting her gaze.

Nimmo loved jalebis more than any sweet. She sat down to taste the first lot of jalebis the cook made when Amaro came and sat down beside her.

"Go ahead and enjoy the jalebis while you can, sister, you hardly know what is in store for you," said Amaro dramatically, drawing a long breath and hastily looking over her shoulder to check that no one was eavesdropping.

"What are you talking about?" Nimmo looked bewildered as her heart skipped a beat, the jalebi in her hand frozen midway to her mouth.

"Have you heard nothing at all? Look, sister, I have no role in this. I have been so upset and tried my best to dissuade Bebe. But when does she ever listen to me? And this crafty Bhua is the one who is the root of all evil. Who can change destiny anyway? Look at my own massi's daughter from Jalalabad…"

"Please don't talk in riddles," Nimmo interrupted anxiously. "My heart is sinking. Tell me what you mean? What has happened?"

"You know it has been difficult to find a groom for Rano. Who will accept a squint-eyed shrew? Bebe has made a watta-satta marriage deal with the Nabha sardars family. They are accepting Rano for their son in return for Hukum Singh's marriage to their elder daughter Hansa."

Nimmo felt the blood drain from her body and could hardly find her voice. "Hai hai, what are you saying? How can they do this? Don't they know he is married?"

"Of course they do. But they also know that you have failed to have a child. Their girl has crossed the marriageable age because she insisted on studying up to college, and they could not find an equally educated and well-placed Jat boy for her. They have been assured that you will live here in the village and she will live with Hukum. And, I hear that their son is an opium addict, and they couldn't find a girl from a good family for him either. So they have agreed for Rano's match for him and ignored her squint. Both families have made an exchange agreement."

"But have they asked Hukum Singh? Has he agreed?" asked Nimmo in a small voice.

"Why would he refuse? Don't you understand men yet? He is getting an educated woman who will give him a child and be able to sit and stand with his officer friends and bade sahibs. I hear she is very fair and pretty too. He has all his five fingers in ghee."

Amaro had always resented Nimmo for being lucky enough to marry her fauji brother-in-law and accompany him to the city whereas she was destined to stay in the village with her boorish husband, serving her in-laws and milking the buffaloes. She found a perverse satisfaction in welcoming Nimmo to the same scenario.

Forcing her shock-paralyzed body to lift up slowly, Nimmo walked into the house in a stupefied state, unable to grasp the reality of what had been told to her. She confronted her mother-in-law in the kitchen.

"Bebe, have you have found a second wife for your son?"

Jeeti averted her eyes and continued chopping saag.

"Answer me! Why are you quiet?" Nimmo screamed hysterically.

"Yes. So what have we done which has not been done before? This is the way of the world. Must you think only of yourself? You have given my son no children. And how were we to show our face in the community with a daughter as high as the roof sitting on our chest? Is this the first time a man has taken a second wife? We are not turning you out of the house. You will stay with us and get all you need. All this is destiny. Can I rewrite your destiny now? I also came into this house as the second wife of Hukum's bapu. I even had to tolerate my sauken who lived in the same house and lorded over me as long as she lived. After her death, I had to raise her son, who treats me like dirt now. You at least will not stay with her in the same house. Don't take it to heart. Hukum will keep visiting you here."

"I curse all of you and your son, who are going to do this injustice to me! May you all not find a place even in hell! You had better stop this marriage right now, or I will curse your entire family, and kill myself by jumping off the roof!" Tears were streaming down Nimmo's face as she collapsed on the floor.

"Control yourself, girl! Realize your position! Go kill yourself if you must and be damned. What will you do if we turn you out and send you back to your parents' house? What will the community say about you and who will accept your younger sister's match? Everyone knows you are a childless hag. Is my son to stay childless too because you are a barren woman? He is a big afsar and can get any woman he points to. You have an option to stay here quietly or return to your parents' home if you so wish."

Bhua heard the altercation and stepped in with her own advice.

"Girl, you have married into the Raikot Sardars' family. They are known to take a second wife if they do not like the nose of the first one! Who do you think you are? Will our son carry the curse of your barrenness? Look at my sister-in-law—she became ill with a fever which would not go away. She herself got her husband married to her aunt's daughter, and they are all happy. What use is a woman who cannot provide an heir to the family? And it's not like you are very beautiful or educated either. Calm down and accept your destiny. This is Waheguru's will."

Rano's was married off with a hefty dowry which included much of Nimmo's jewellery, twenty-one beddings packed in three sandooks with elaborate inlay work, fifty-one utensils, sixteen suits, six phulkaris, a gold kantha and kara for her husband and several sets of clothing for her in-laws. A milk buffalo was sent along too.

That night, Nimmo lay on her bed exhausted and drained with a feeling of having lost all she had. She could see nothing but darkness ahead. What would she do? Where would she go? In one swift blow destiny had robbed her of her identity and status, both drawn from her being a wife to Hukum Singh. Where did she stand now that he had rejected her? Would her parents take her back? She remembered the warnings given to her by Maji, and the disapproval of her parents when her bhua had come home after being beaten by her husband. Bholan had to be married yet. They would not want the stigma of a married daughter coming back home. She spent the night without a wink of sleep, listening to the cicadas piercing the darkness with shrill chirrups, echoing the searing pain in her own heart.

12

Hansa

Hukum Singh's second marriage was a quiet affair. He brought his new wife home as the sun cast golden shadows across the courtyard, and sparrows chirped in the branches of the neem tree. No one paid attention to Nimmo as she stood behind a half-open door and watched the newlyweds step over the threshold.

The bride wore a blazing-red silk lehenga with extensive gota work and a veil with heavy gold zardozi work and broad Benarasi lace. Hukum Singh was resplendent in a white achkan and pink turban, with a gold kalgi, just as when he had come to wed Nimmo, riding a white steed. Donning a pink veil with gota, Jeeti was all smiles as she trickled mustard oil on both sides of the door and swung a water pitcher around the bride and the groom to ward off the evil eye.

Nimmo marvelled bitterly at the fickleness of fate as

tears streamed down her face. Here was the man she had left everything for; the man she was ready to follow to the end of the earth. Just a short time ago she was the one who had stood at the threshold with Hukum Singh, and Bebe had gone through the same ritual for her. But the evil eye had damned her happiness nevertheless!

As Jeeti lifted the long red bridal veil covering Hansa's face, Nimmo saw that she was fair, with soft contours and a pleasant demeanour. Everyone made much of her, exclaiming over her beauty, her jewellery and fine clothes. Sick with pain and anger, Nimmo retreated into her room. In the days that followed, she tried her best to avoid coming face to face with the new bride, surreptitiously gaping at her beautiful, fashionable clothes and stylish jewellery.

Hukum Singh avoided meeting Nimmo. He kept out of the house most of the day, going straight to his room at night. Nimmo wanted to confront him but did not have the courage to do so. This huge blow had broken her spirit. Anyway, what would be the use of asking him anything now? What was done was done.

Hansa moved around the house with inherent confidence which made all the other women a bit bashful and nervous. She was not much the shy bride and spoke freely with the women of the house and visitors. They were all quite overawed by her, and Bebe gave her star treatment. Relatives came visiting to look at the new bride and also to watch Nimmo's reaction; some would offer her hushed, surreptitious sympathies. Nimmo fought hard to keep up a brave front and avoided meeting guests as far as she could.

"Sat Sri Akal behen ji."

Nimmo swung around to face Hansa standing at the door to her room. She was too dumbstruck even to answer, and could only nod her head weakly. Hansa wore a pink silk suit with zari motifs, a long jadau necklace and earrings, and a tikka on her forehead. Her hair was tied back in a stylish bun. She walked in and sat on the chair by the bed. Nimmo stepped away involuntarily, feeling shabby in her old cotton salwar suit. Why had she come? Here was the woman who had snatched away everything from her, and yet she had the audacity to come and speak to her.

"Maybe you are angry with me. Anyone in your place would be angry. But this is all our fate. Can we fight sanjog? I had no more say in my marriage than you had in yours. Do you think I wanted to become a second wife? But now that it is done there is no use carrying venom in our hearts. I mean you no harm. I hope we can live together like sisters."

"You are a witch who has ruined my life. How can you even think that we can live as sisters? May you rot in hell for taking my rights. Get out and don't show me your face again."

Humiliated, Hansa left the room.

Hukum Singh left for Ambala with his new bride. Nimmo would stay here with his parents. Nimmo simmered as she pictured another woman take over a home that she had put together so lovingly; a woman who would now cook in her kitchen and sleep with her husband in her bed.

She sent word to her parents to fetch her. Her mother sent the nain to say that she was heartbroken to hear that her in-laws had brought a sauken over her, but she should adjust and not lose heart. Nimmo understood that she'd have to make peace with her fate and not use her husband's second marriage as a pretext for returning home. Her status in her in-laws home had gone down by many notches by virtue of her being a rejected wife. She felt bitter and resentful towards Bebe Jeeti and Bhua for having brought sauken in the house and her relationship with them deteriorated considerably. She often snapped at them out of frustration, and they retaliated by assigning her the toughest duties of milking and bathing the buffaloes and grinding wheat into flour on a heavy stone grinding wheel. She was embarrassed to meet women in the village and found herself isolated and lonely. There was no one she could share her grief with. Bau ji was the only family member who was kind to her. But what comfort could she draw from an ailing, weak old man who himself had little say in the house and looked to her for succour and aid. Amaro even seemed to have tutored Guddi against her, who started avoiding her on the pretext of studying.

Meanwhile, she noticed that Bachana had started to pay her extra attention.

"If you need anything, you just have to ask me. Don't feel shy," he said to her one day as he came to the kitchen to get some water. Nimmo was thankful for the sympathy. Once she fell ill and was running a high fever, and it was Bachana who took her to the hakim and got her treated. He even bought her a new suit when he returned from a trip to the city. This gesture did not go well with Amaro, who started eyeing her with even more suspicion and hostility after that.

One stormy, summer day Amaro's uncle came to fetch

her with the news that she had lost her father. Bachana told Amaro to leave with the children, staying back on the pretext of running a fever.

"I will join you in a day or two as soon as I am well enough to travel," he said.

Next day Jeeti and Bhua collected women relatives from the village and proceeded to Amaro's village for makaan, leaving behind Nimmo to look after the house and cattle.

A death in the family was a momentous occasion. It was an event for community gathering and elaborate religious rituals. Old men or women, much neglected during their last years, would be passionately mourned after death. Jeeti led a group of women in billowing white and black ghagras to Amaro's village, laughing and chatting along the way. As soon as they arrived within earshot of the house, they quickly drew down veils on their faces and let out long heart-rending wails.

Mourning was nothing less than a cultural art. It was both a tribute to the deceased as well as a cathartic exercise for the bereaved family. When they entered Amaro's parent's house, the mirasan accompanying them initiated long drawn out wails of siapa, the rest of the women following her lead. She had a talented voice and poetic inclination, putting together mournful rhymes on the spot. With white cotton veils drawn low over their faces, the women sang dirges to the departed in perfect unison, wrenching out tears from the eyes of the most stoic in the gathering.

"Hai sardar ji, where have you gone betraying the woman you had brought home in a doli!"

"Hai sardar ji, why have you snatched away the red

dupatta of suhaag from her head and left her bereft to cry forever!"

"Hai sardar ji, why have you left your palace deserted and forlorn?"

"Who will take care of your vast properties and estates now?"

Once inside the house, they formed a circle around the widow, beating their chests in rhythm to wails, and striking her on the back as they lamented her bad luck.

Back in Raipur, Nimmo tried to get her evening chores done as strong gusts of wind whistled through the Pipal tree, and an open window swung crazily against the wall. A vessel fell from a kitchen shelf and rumbled on to the floor. A stray dog howled in the street, and soon others took up his call. Bau ji had gone to bed. Nimmo was trying to light a lantern against the strong wind when she felt a hand on her shoulder. Startled, she swung around to find Bachana facing her with a possessed look in his eyes. He took the unlighted lantern from her hands and put it away, pulling her close. It took a few moments for Nimmo to register this unexpected assault.

"What are you doing? Are you out of your mind? Let go of me," said Nimmo nervously.

"Hush, don't raise your voice. It's okay. Come with me. Look at you; left alone in the prime of youth. But never mind, I will take care of you. You don't have to worry about anything."

Nimmo could smell liquor on his breath as he pressed her to his thick, burly, body and greedily ran his hands over her breasts and buttocks.

"You are drunk. You don't know what you are doing.

Let me go, or I will scream and wake up Bau ji."

Bachana caught hold of her hair and shook her violently.

"Who do you think you are? Your husband has left you. Nobody cares about you here. I am the one who spoke up for you to be allowed to stay here; otherwise, you would have been kicked out of this house. Do you think your parents will take you back and suffer a social embarrassment when they still have another daughter to marry off? I thought you would be thankful to me for watching your interests, and you are showing me a temper instead? You had better learn to listen to me, or you will be out begging in the streets. Anyway, what difference does it make? I am not an outsider but your husband's elder brother," he leered, breathing heavily.

Nimmo tried to resist as she was half-dragged to his room. But Bachana was large and strong, and she didn't stand a chance. She tried to scream as he tore away at her clothes but was silenced with a stinging slap across her face.

"Who is here to hear you now? And, if you think of making any allegations against me, I will tell everyone that it was you who came to my room. Who do you think they will believe—you or me? Come on now, be a good girl. Don't let me hit you again," he said, squeezing her breast hard and biting into her shoulder.

Exhausted into submission, Nimmo went limp and silently bore the assaults on her body. Bruised and humiliated, she dragged herself to her room, sobbing and trying to come to terms with the trauma. After regaining some of her strength, she went to bathe, spending a long time in soaping and scrubbing herself.

Jeeti and Amaro returned the next day, and the house reverted to its usual routine. But Nimmo's life had changed and was never to be the same again. Bachan Singh managed to find occasional opportunities to ravish her. Maybe it was more than just sex. He had always suffered the humiliation of being the unwanted son. Losing his mother at an early age had left him largely unattended and ignored, and Jeeti had treated him as a burden and a nuisance. His father never hid his disappointment in him for his dark complexion, ungainly looks and average intelligence. Naib Singh focused all his affections on Hukum Singh, who was better than him in all respects—he was handsome, did well in studies and went on to become an officer—while Bachana could not grasp the written word and was relegated to farming. He was married to a dowdy-looking uneducated girl from a low-placed family, while Hukum Singh was lucky enough to get two wives. Sleeping with Hukum Singh's wife gave him a perverse satisfaction of getting even for all the injustices meted out to him.

Nimmo knew that there was no sympathy for her in this family, no one she could confide in. No one would believe her if she complained against Bachana. So she came to accept these sexual assaults for fear of being beaten and accused. It is amazing how much the human mind will adjust to—something utterly shocking and repulsive can slowly gain acceptability when there is no escape from it. Adaptability is often the only key to survival, and no one knows it better than women. She became withdrawn and sullen. A feeling of guilt and self-loathing kept her from visiting her parents.

During summers, the rooftops came alive in the evenings as people made their way up to escape the stifling heat in the confined spaces of houses. Most of the village houses were built in a cluster with interconnected roofs, and on lucky days, one could hope for a refreshing cool breeze from the northern hills. As dusk set in, mud-plastered roofs were cooled by sprinkling water, and string cots pulled up for the night. It was a specialized exercise in which one person held up the light weight cot against the wall, pushing it up towards the roof edge, while another one positioned himself on the roof to pull it up. Beddings were spread out, and a terracotta pitcher of water placed on the side. Villagers would wind up the evening chores and ascend to the cooler roof. Now and then, someone would start telling a story about Laila Majnu or Shirin Farhaad, and everyone would listen with rapt attention. The story session would generally last till the nine o'clock train rumbled past with a long, piercing whistle, which would be a signal for the storyteller to wind up and continue the narration the next evening.

Rooftops also afforded an opportunity for youngsters to flirt and fool around. Bachana's daughter Guddi had turned fourteen and started paying extra attention to her looks and clothes. She loved to borrow clothes from Nimmo and tried lining her eyes with kohl. Bebe Jeeti often chastised her for spending too much time for her toilet. Nimmo had noticed that she took an extraordinary interest in the Pandit's son in the neighbourhood, often hanging around the door to peek at him when it was time for him to leave for school. She also saw them exchange smiles as they crossed each other in the street.

One evening when the women were preparing dinner, Guddi was sent to the roof to spread beddings on the cots. The family was shocked to see Bachana drag down a screaming Guddi by the hair.

"I shall teach you how to make eyes at boys. I shall kill you and bury you in this very courtyard before you smear ashes on my face, you ill-begotten girl," he yelled, slapping and kicking her viciously. The women were all aghast and rushed to ask what had happened.

"I suspected that she and the Pandit's boy have something going on between them, so I decided to check today. Sure enough, this bitch was laughing and talking with him across the roof. I will go and tackle that haramzada also, but first I will finish her." Amaro tried to intervene and was slapped hard, which sent her reeling.

"You are responsible for taking care of your daughter," yelled Bachana, "What have you been doing while she was playing with the family's honour? Are you blind that you do not know what is happening under your very nose?"

Bebe Jeeti did not intervene, watching quietly from the side. Guddi started bleeding from the nose as Bachana kept hitting her in frenzied anger. Nimmo could restrain herself no more. She rushed and caught his arm and said in a steely voice, "It's enough. Stop right now. She is only a child. Everyone makes mistakes. And if you confront the boy you will only create a drama for the village to enjoy."

Supporting Guddi, she took her aside to wash her face and give her some water to drink.

How different the moral codes are for men and women, Nimmo thought. Hypocritical bastards! Why are women alone custodians of the so-called honour of the family? Why are men entitled to all the pleasures of the flesh without endangering this honour? When it takes two to play the game, how come it was justified for them to force themselves on women but forbidden for women to even speak with other males? She wished she had the courage to confront him with these questions, but knew she could not. Women had accepted these anomalies quietly since centuries, and so would she.

13

Black Magic

Dussehra was just two days away, and people were busy cleaning their houses, plastering mud floors and walls afresh with a mixture of white clay and cow dung. The Goddess Kali was depicted and worshipped as 'Sanjhi', especially to get good husbands for unmarried girls, and women tried to outdo each other in decorating house walls with images of Sanjhi in lime and charcoal.

Amaro and Nimmo had sowed barley seeds in earthen pots on the first day of Navratras, and embedded barley saplings in Bau ji's and Naib Singh's turbans to bring them luck. It was an era of blissful ignorance and innocence about the distilled purity of Sikhism and Hinduism, and people owned and celebrated a mixture of traditions and festivals from both religions, without any sense of proprietorship of one or a feeling of the 'other'. People were simple, and their demands from gods, goddesses, saints, fakirs and divine elements were basic; they asked for a good harvest, milk-producing cattle, sons, health and welfare for the family. Any deity who may grant these wishes was worthy of being prayed to, offered whatever gifts he/she was partial to, and pampered with rituals and festivals in his/her honour. It was plain and simple give and take, with no philosophical or spiritual ambitions. All that was to come later with the Singh Sabha and Arya Samaj preachers.

A tonga came to a halt in the narrow paved lane in front of the haveli, a couple of children following it curiously. Hukum Singh climbed out followed by Hansa, looking pretty in a beautiful green-and-mauve printed salwar suit. She wore high-heeled sandals on her feet and carried a handbag. Bebe Jeeti and Amaro hastened to receive them. Unlike the other daughters-in-law, Hansa did not bow down to touch her in-laws' feet but folded her hands and wished them with a Sat Sri Akal.

"Put on the tea, Nimmo," Bebe Jeeti instructed as she hugged Hansa and bestowed a string of blessings on her. Nimmo retreated into the kitchen, her heart beating wildly inside her chest. She could not bear to face Hukum Singh. Would he look at her and know of her transgressions?

"Sat Sri Akal, Behenji," said Hansa, coming up to Nimmo. Murmuring a grudging reply, Nimmo left it at that, pretending to be occupied with making tea.

The Sanjhi idol that had adorned the mud wall of the house for the last nine days was scraped off on Dashmi to be immersed in water. Later in the evening, Bebe Jeeti, along with Amaro, Bhua and Hansa, joined the procession of women headed towards the village pond to immerse Sanjhi in water. They carried the idols in baskets placed on their heads, along with small clay lamps twinkling in the evening light, and sang simple devotional songs on the way. Nimmo had prayed and offered food to the Goddess every evening for the last nine days. She made excuses to stay back, and no one insisted that she go.

When her mother Chinti had visited, she had coached her to try and win her way back into Hukum Singh's heart by hook or by crook. This was her chance to find him alone. She took care to dress up in a clean suit, combed her hair carefully and lined her eyes with kohl. Nimmo laid out some saag and makki roti in a large brass plate, with some pickled green chillies and raw onion on the side. She had prepared some sewiyan for him; undoing a small wrapper tied to the corner of her dupatta, she mixed some white powder into the bowl.

"I have brought your dinner ji."

She laid the plate in front of Hukum Singh and pulled a peehri to sit down close to his chair. Feeling uncomfortable on being alone with her, Hukum Singh quickly started eating to cover the awkwardness. Nimmo looked hard at him.

"You have become a total stranger to me. Do you ever think of how I live? What did I do to deserve this punishment? Did I ever disobey you or refuse you anything? You should have strangled me with your own hands before bringing a sauken in front of my eyes." She broke down in sobs.

"Don't start wailing now. Am I dead? What have I done that has not been done before? Am I the first Sardar to have two wives? What harm have I done to God that I do not have a son to carry on my name? I have a certain status in society and the army. You are uneducated and don't know how to move in an educated society, and I still put up with it. But is it my fault that you are barren? And I have responsibilities towards my sister too. Could I refuse my elders? It is not that you have been thrown out of the house and sent back to your parent's house. You are being fed and clothed. What more do you want?"

He continued with his dinner as Nimmo wiped her eyes with her dupatta and fetched him a glass of water. She removed the empty plate from the table with a sense of achievement. She had managed to feed him the maulvi's taveet—there was hope for her. Her mother had made a special trip to the old Muslim town of Malerkotla to meet the maulvi. He was known to be an expert in the knowledge of the 'Lal Kitab'—a famous age-old paranormal text dealing with astrological planetary afflictions and their remedies, brought about by making certain potions or taveet, imbued with the power of certain magical verses. Chinti had given two separate taveet to her, to feed to her husband and his second wife. She added the powder to Hansa's bowl of sewiyan too.

Next morning Nimmo carried breakfast for Hukum Singh to his room. Her mother had specially instructed her to try and stay around him when he came home. She was taken aback to see him lying listlessly on the bed, with Hansa sitting beside him and wiping his forehead with a towel.

"What has happened to him?" asked Nimmo.

"He has had diarrhoea all night and breaks into a cold

141

sweat every now and then. Let's take him to the doctor," replied Hansa in a worried voice. She seemed drowsy and heavy-lidded too.

"Let's wait for a while. I will give him some ajwain. Probably it's nothing serious, just something he ate on the train. You just go and lie down now. I will take care of him," Nimmo spoke nicely to her for the first time.

"Maybe you are right. We had some pakore in the train. I am feeling very drowsy too. I can't sit up straight."

Hukum Singh lay weak and spent for the entire day as Nimmo fussed around him, feeding him yoghurt and lassi, massaging his feet and fanning him. She was worried about the effect of the taveet on him but did not want to lose this opportunity to reconnect with her husband. Hansa slept through the day, inviting many snide remarks from Bebe and Amaro for neglecting her ill husband. Hukum Singh recovered, but Hansa continued to be unwell.

Nimmo took pains over dressing up well, doing her hair nicely, wearing jewellrey and lining her eyes with kohl. Hansa was starting to get visibly uncomfortable about Nimmo's hanging around her husband but could do little with her continued state of drowsiness, and frequent vomiting, induced by a daily dose of taveet slipped surreptitiously into her food. It made it necessary for her to place her cot near the drain out in the yard at night. She began to get suspicious and refused to accept any eatable from Nimmo, but the damage was done. Nimmo had been surreptitiously visiting Hukum Singh's room for the last four nights. Hukum Singh, of course, felt that it was his right to have access to both his wives, and Hansa should make her peace with it. Working in the kitchen that evening,

Nimmo smirked as she heard the sound of a quarrel from Hukum Singh's room, followed by Hansa's wailing. She prayed that she would be able to give Hukum Singh a child soon. That would be her only redemption.

14

Destiny Knocks

Nimmo had been feeling out of sorts. She felt nauseous in the mornings and threw up a couple of times. Jeeti promptly summoned the village midwife, who confirmed that Nimmo was pregnant. Something had finally worked; whether it was the peer's taveet or her supplications at the gurudwara, she couldn't say, but fate had favoured her over Hansa. She visited all the local deities and prayed for a son to reinstate her position in the family. Sardar Naib Singh and Jeeti were ecstatic.

"May you live long, bahu! May your husband and brother enjoy long lives! Waheguru has finally answered my prayers. May He bless you with many sons and abundance of milk!"

Jeeti and others started treating her with new respect and concern, paying extra attention to her diet and making sure she received milk and ghee in plenty. Bindo was instructed to massage her legs and back.

"Nee Amaro, why can you not wash those clothes? Can't you see that Nimmo needs to get some rest? Bindo, fetch her a glass of milk."

Relieved of household duties, Nimmo often found time to go and sit next to Bau ji, listening to his tales of yester-years with fascination.

"My bapu had joined as a havaldar in the Angrezi fauj. He fought and died in Mosul in 1916 during the First World War, so the sarkar awarded him a tagma and fifty acres of land in Montgomery. They named the town Montgomery after the angrez Laat sahib of Punjab who developed it. Lyallpur too was named after the gora Laat sahib Lyall. Do you know of Sargodha, your mother-in-law's peke?"

Nimmo shook her head. Her knowledge of the world was limited to her village, her bhua's village, Ludhiana and Ambala.

"It is inhabited mostly by fauji afsars who were awarded jagirs by the angrez for their faithful service in the wars. The Maharani in vilayat is very generous in rewarding people who are loyal and serve her well. The rajahs of Patiala, Nabha and Faridkot were made jarnails for their support in the two World Wars. I was very keen that Naib should join the army, but it did not happen. Now I am happy that Hukum has realized my dream."

"But Bau ji, on the other hand, he says that the angrez sarkar did not allow Indians to travel in any but the third class in trains? Neither were they allowed to enter clubs till recently. Why did they treat us like untouchables?" asked Nimmo.

"They are the hakam, daughter. How can we be equal to them? Rajas and their parja cannot be at the same level. It has been so for centuries."

Confident of her improved status, Nimmo refused to pander to Bachana's randy demands any longer, and he realized it was time to back off. Hukum Singh, elated with the news of her pregnancy, started visiting her more often. He was happy with Hansa and proud of her sophistication and good looks, but somewhere deep down, the strong aspiration for a son overrode every other feeling. She had not borne him a child either, and it gave him a feeling of shameful inadequacy and incompleteness, making him feel less of a man. Nimmo earned a new status in his eyes now that she was carrying his child. He started spending more time with her, bringing her gifts of new clothes and sweets. One evening, just as he was drifting off to sleep after a session of lovemaking, Nimmo held his face and turned it towards her.

"Listen ji. I want to come to Ambala with you," she demanded with her newfound confidence.

"What are you talking about? Go to sleep now. Don't start making absurd demands. You know it's not possible."

"Why? Why is it not possible? Am I not your legally wedded wife? Is that witch the only one destined to enjoy your bungalow and thath-baat while I perish here in the village slaving for your family?" She sat up in bed now, heaving and shouting in a high-pitched voice.

"This memsaab of yours has not been able to give you a child, has she? What use is she with her painted lips and high heels like a kanjari?

Hukum Singh was taken aback by this new avatar of

Nimmo. She had never been so bold and aggressive before.

"Stop screaming and cursing like a madwoman! Don't lose your head if I have given you some importance. You know Hansa will not allow you in my house. I don't want to turn my life to hell with two women squabbling all the time. Do you lack anything here? Tell me, and I will get it for you."

"Oh, so this big soldier is afraid and cowers with fear in front of that scheming woman! You are a slave to that whore's fair skin, aren't you?"

Hukum Singh slapped her across the face.

"Shut up you haramzadi, and get out of here! Your tongue has suddenly grown very long! Don't forget that my sister is married to her brother. I cannot annoy Hansa and have my sister come back to sit at our doorstep. Just because I am nice to you, are you trying to sit on my head now?"

Nimmo did not cry. She stood up, smoothed back her hair and looked hard at him with blazing eyes.

"If you want to see your child's face, he will be born in the Military Hospital in Ambala. The dai has already told me that the baby is positioned upside down with the cord around his neck. She has refused to perform this delivery. It is for you to decide whether you want your child's life or pander to your memsahib's whims!"

Drawing her dupatta resolutely around her shoulders, she walked out of his room, feeling that she could finally dictate some terms in her marriage. She would soon be the mother of a son, God willing, and reclaim her position as Hukum Singh's first wife. Now she could take on Hansa, her husband's memsahib.

Nimmo's mother sent for her when informed about her pregnancy. It was customary for girls to come to their parental homes for deliveries.

"Waheguru's blessings on you, daughter; my ardas and mannats have brought about a change in your destiny. You will finally grow roots in your house. A childless woman is cursed to live the life of a chattel."

Bholan had been engaged to the son of a well-to-do jagirdar family in Patiala. Her would-be father-in-law was a courtier to the Maharaja Patiala. Bholan was as excited and elated as Nimmo was before her marriage, and would not stop telling her all about her in-laws and fiancé. Nimmo hoped her happiness would not be as short-lived as hers. She could not see Nama Chacha anywhere around and asked Chinti about him.

"His mental health deteriorated, and he had to be sent to the mental asylum in Amritsar," said Chinti, quickly changing the topic.

"I hope Kaka Hukum Singh is happy now that he will be a father soon. Is he going to take you with him to Ambala now? How is your sauken? Be wary of her. I hope she does not trouble you?" she asked about Hansa.

"They are all fine and treat me much better," said Nimmo. "I need not worry about anyone now that I am going to be the mother of his child. Why does the house seem so quiet, Bebe? Bapu ji must be in the fields, but where is Maji? I have not heard her voice ever since I have come, and she can hardly stay quiet for so long."

"She is a little unwell and resting in her room. Let her be; you can meet her later."

Ignoring her, Nimmo went inside to Maji's room. The

windows were shut, leaving the room in semi-darkness and smelling dank. Maji lay on her bed, looking weak and ill.

"What's wrong with you, Maji? You look so ill," Nimmo anxiously asked as she bent down to hug and greet her.

Maji's lips trembled without answering her greetings, and tears trickled down her face. Nimmo tried to talk to her, but she would not respond. Nimmo could not get anything out of her mother either, but she could sense that something was very wrong. She took Jamalo aside and asked her what was wrong with Maji.

"Biba ji, she has been affected deeply ever since Zaildar Sahib sent away Nama sardar to the hospital. She is a mother, after all. Don't ask me to say anything further. It's not my place to comment on elders. Allah will have mercy on him," whispered Jamalo.

Nimmo went back to Maji's room and sat by her bedside, holding her wrinkled hands in her own.

"Maji, I can understand that you are upset with Chacha being sent to the mental hospital, but I am told his condition had worsened and he had become violent. He could have hurt someone or even himself. There was no option. Please do not take this to heart. He is being treated there and will soon recover and return home."

The old woman let out a pitiful wail.

"He will never recover and return home. His condition did not worsen on its own. He was constantly fed with slow poison to destabilize his brain. My son was a simpleton but totally fine." She wailed on.

Nimmo was shocked and speechless for a while.

"What are you saying Maji? But who has been

poisoning him? And why?"

"My womb is cursed. I can blame no one else. Kehar Singh is the one who has been doing this to his younger brother. Since he does not have a son, he was afraid that if Nama got married and had a son, the entire family land would go to him. So he has been feeding him slow poison and traumatizing him for many years, making sure that he is mentally impaired and not capable of getting married. Nama has been reduced to a state where he is not even capable of asking for his own share of land now."

"But how can you be so sure?"

"The doctor in the hospital said so. I had shown him the medicine which Kehar used to give Nama. The doctor said it was opium which damaged the brain when given over time. Kehar beat Nama and forced him to take the medicine when he resisted. Whenever I would try to intervene to stop Kehar from beating him, he would push me aside, saying that he was giving him medicine for his good and that Nama was mad and would turn violent and hit people if not given the medicine. I believed him because Nama would suddenly calm down and get drowsy after taking medicine. Little did I know that he was being given high doses of opium. I have failed to protect him as a mother and allowed him to be destroyed in front of my eyes. I can never forgive Kehar for his atrocities on his brother. I never suspected that he could be so heartless and avaricious."

Nimmo could barely absorb the blow of this terrifying revelation about her father. It now became clear to Nimmo why Nama Chacha had been so scared of him. Another pillar of trust in her life fell and shattered. Her father, whom she had so looked up to, was capable of slowly poisoning his own flesh and blood to grab his share of land.

Zaildar Kehar Singh was out on a trip to Ludhiana. In a state of disbelief and shock, Nimmo went and accosted her mother, repeating Maji's accusations. Chinti tried to deny them, saying she knew nothing, but Nimmo could sense that she was lying. She sent for the rathwan.

"I cannot stay in a house where such violence and injustice is being done. Please tell Bapu ji that I never want to set foot here again and want nothing from this house. It is tainted with blood and evil. I am going back."

Chinti tried to stop her, but Nimmo left without looking back.

15

Bungalows and Bugles

Hansa loved her life as an army wife. It was an exciting and sophisticated lifestyle unique to the army. The cantonment was a world within a world offering the best facilities anyone could have. Officers and soldiers were trained to follow basic discipline and etiquette in behaviour, dress and demeanour, which dictated courtesy to women at all times and in every way. Hansa was flattered when senior officers rose to wish her, regardless of rank. She marvelled at the commitment of the British officers' wives to welfare activities in the unit, which was like a large family in many ways. They invested a lot of time and energy in connecting with wives of junior ranks through the welfare centres, training them in stitching, tailoring and cooking, and attending to any personal problems that they might share. Wives cooperated in knitting sweaters, socks and caps for the soldiers posted in hostile and cold mountainous regions.

Being well-educated and conversant in English, Hansa played an active role in the regiment. During a welfare meeting with the Commanding Officer's wife, Mrs Gillespie, a JCO's wife came up with a complaint against her husband, which Hansa translated into English for her.

"She says that he comes home drunk most evenings and beats her up for trivial things. She cannot bear the beatings but has nowhere else to go."

"How come no one has been monitoring his liquor bills? Please tell her that I will ask CO Sahib to look into his liquor intake and also issue him a warning. He will not touch her again." said Mrs Gillespie, reassuring the woman.

Hansa had developed a good rapport with other officers' wives and participated enthusiastically in assisting Major Thomson's wife in preparing for the upcoming Annual Regimental Sports Day. Trophies were to be laid out, seating and tea arrangements supervised. Sport in the army was more than just entertainment—it played an important role in keeping up the morale of sepoys and officers, and was greatly encouraged. It brought together men from varying backgrounds and developed a team spirit in them, besides keeping them physically fit and away from alcohol and prostitution.

"Keep the boys busy and on the go if you want to keep them out of mischief! Better they exhaust their energy riding a four-legged mare than two-legged ones in the Laal Bazaar!" said Mrs. Gillespie wickedly, sending the women into peals of laughter.

Being active at sports came to symbolize Britishness

and vigour, and officers who did not participate in a sport were looked down upon as being that much of lesser men. Divisional tournaments were organized with much pomp, the most popular sports being polo, hockey, football, tent pegging, tug of war, javelin throw and races. The best unit carried off the much-coveted trophy. Hunting excursions were another favourite pastime for officers, and very often they were accompanied by their wives for elaborately orchestrated hunts. Hansa had learnt horse riding and hunting and often accompanied Hukum Singh and other officers for hunting trips.

The regimental stadium was a pretty sight with its running tracks marked with precise slaked lime lines and coloured flags fluttering gaily in the autumn breeze. The path leading up to the stadium was spread in red soil, with rows of potted marigolds lining the sides. Lower parts of tree trunks were painted red and white. Rows of chairs were lined up for the spectators under colourful shamianas, and senior officers and their wives sat in the front row, strictly according to rank. Most of them were British, with their wives turned out smartly in calf-length dresses, hats and sunglasses. However much they sheltered themselves against the harsh Punjab sun, they ended up with a million brown freckles on their faces. There were a couple of Indian officers, their wives in elegant chiffon saris or smart salwar kameez. The officers were turned out smartly in civvies and shiny brogues.

Hansa stood out for her attractive looks and demeanour. She wore an onion pink georgette sari which added a warm glow to her fair complexion. Her long black hair was neatly tied back in a low bun, with a pink rose tucked in at the side. She wore a string of pearls on her neck and pearl studs in her ears.

The events included races, javelin throw, tug-of-war and amazing daredevil feats on motorcycles. Uniformed bearers donning be-ribboned turbans, white coats with cummerbunds and long white gloves, served cold lemonade. Mrs Gillespie gave away the prizes to the winners. The event was followed by high tea, and Mrs Thomson thanked Hansa for her assistance in organizing the event. Hansa was ebullient as she accompanied Hukum Singh home, humming a popular filmi song.

"The event went really well, don't you think? Mrs Thomson was so happy with me. Twice she said 'Thank you, thank you' to me. She is very nice with no airs about her."

"Hmmm," replied Hukum Singh distractedly.

"So many women complimented me for my sari today, and you had nothing to say at all," she pouted.

"It looks very nice."

Hansa started to undo her saree with slow and provocative movements, plucking out the pleats one by one and pirouetting to display her bare midriff and shapely breasts in a well-fitted short blouse, swaying her hips to Suraiya's popular song:

"Tu mera chaand maen teri chandni, ho...o"

She threw one end of her sari at Hukum Singh and batted her eyelashes seductively.

Hukum Singh looked away.

"Hanso, I have something important to discuss with you."

"Yes?"

"You know Nimmo is pregnant?"

"So?"

Her dancing came to a halt, and she sobered up. It was a sore point that Hansa constantly tried to push to the back of her mind.

"She wants to come here for the delivery."

Hansa turned sharply to look him in the eye. Her high spirits deflated like a pricked balloon.

"I thought it was understood that this is my house; that she would never set foot here. Is it not enough that I have to live with the pain of having a sauken that now you want to bring her and place her on my head? Do you want to rub it in my face that she is going to give you a child now while I have not conceived..." she broke into sobs.

"Don't think about yourself alone. What about the welfare of the child? How can you be so selfish? Will not my child be yours too? I am not keen to bring her here any more than you are. But I cannot risk the child's life. You know there is no medical help in the village except for that old midwife who can hardly see properly. The baby is positioned upside down with the cord around his neck. Anything can go wrong. Who will be responsible then? Here we have the best medical facilities in the Military hospital. This is not for her. It is for the safety of my child—our child."

Hansa had held many misgivings about becoming a second wife to an already married man. But having crossed twenty-four, she was way beyond the age of finding a suitable, unmarried match, unless it were someone with a defect. It might seem strange, but Hansa's beauty and education were, in fact, responsible for her not having found a befitting man. The average Jat Sikh girl did not study beyond primary or middle school, and was married off between 16 to 18 years of age. Few went to college. Hansa had a progressive father who had encouraged her to do her masters. By the time she finished her degree, her parents could not find an equally educated and well-placed match for her in the Jat Sikh community. The only choice seemed to be to marry her off to a widower with children or as a second wife. Their son had turned an opium addict due to an easy life and much pampering, making it difficult to find a good wife for him. Hansa's father was a jagirdar from the royal state of Nabha and proud of his ancestry. There was no way that he could marry his children below his status. Thus when Pandit Sewa Ram suggested a watta-satta marriage which would take care of both unions at one go, he reluctantly agreed. It seemed that there was no better choice for his son and daughter. Hansa was very distressed when told of her father's decision, but it was not for her to choose. Moreover, her brother's marriage was to be considered too.

Hansa was a good-natured woman who had acquired some maturity of thought through her education. She could empathize with Nimmo's pain for being rejected and did not want to see her as an adversary. She knew Nimmo did not have much education, beauty or style, neither had she been able to give an heir to Hukum Singh. It was common for men to marry again if the first wife was barren. Confident of her attributes, Hansa knew that Nimmo would be no competition to her, making it easier for her to be the larger person. Hansa decided that she would have a cordial relationship with Nimmo, but that they would never stay together.

However, Hansa had not conceived even after two years of her marriage. Much as she missed motherhood, she felt quite secure with Hukum Singh. He adored her, and she led a privileged life with no time to mope. Something was always going on in the regiment. There were annual flower arrangement shows at the Gymkhana, Mahjong sessions on Wednesdays, Welfare Center meetings and cooking competitions. There were dinners for officers who had been posted out or posted into the station. Hansa stood out with her confidence, looks and charm, making her a much sought after lady. She was an asset to Hukum Singh in a setup where wives were expected to be very visible. Hukum Singh denied her nothing. She had the best of chiffons and silks, pashminas and imported velvets. She had succeeded in pushing Nimmo to the back of her mind, secure in the knowledge that her husband loved her. She was happy in her world in Ambala, and Nimmo was in the village. They did not interfere with each other. Now suddenly she found herself under threat: her home, her fairytale world would be invaded. Hansa was unable to sleep or eat through the two days that Hukum Singh went to the village to fetch Nimmo.

16

The Other Woman

Hansa peeped out of the window as she heard the gate creak open. Hukum Singh helped a heavily pregnant Nimmo climb down from the jeep and called out to the orderly to bring in her luggage. She seemed to be in good health, with a resplendent glow on her young face that expectant mothers have. Hansa avoided going out to greet them, tinkering around aimlessly in the kitchen to control her awkwardness.

Nimmo paused for a while to look at the house wistfully. The lawn was a rich green, surrounded with neat beds of lilies, phlox and petunia. The frangipani trees next to the garage were in full bloom, a pair of squirrels chasing each other up and down its trunk. This was the house where she had imagined her children would play, the house Hukum Singh, the man she had married and loved, had thrown her out of. Another woman ruled this house now, brought over by her husband, making it alien to her. She entered as a guest today, not the owner that she had been. Forsaken by her husband, Nimmo had been reduced to a nonentity.

Following Hukum Singh through the front door, she found that the house looked nothing like she had left it. It was a proper sahib's home with embroidered cushions on upholstered sofas, vilayati pictures on the wall and nicely arranged fresh flowers in cut glass vases. Lace curtains hung on the windows, and there was a Kashmiri carpet on the floor. A long-haired, golden dog ambled up lazily to sniff her. Nimmo froze in fright.

"Sat Sri Akal, behen. Let me show you to your room. You must be tired. I will just send you some tea," said Hansa, taking the dog by his collar.

Nimmo noticed that her eyes were swollen red from crying. She mumbled a reply and followed her.

Hukum Singh was not the kind to question the set order. He went along with tradition, convinced that men were inherently entitled to special privileges. He was used to being pampered and made to feel special in his family because of his good looks, education and status. His mother's suggestion to find him a second wife had been more than welcome, and he was unbothered by any guilt. Hansa was a much better match for his status than Nimmo, and he saw his second marriage as righting of a wrong. Moreover, his sister's marriage was his responsibility too. If one could hit two targets with one arrow, what could be better? But fate had played a trick. Hansa had failed to conceive after two years of marriage, whereas Nimmo was now going to give him an heir. He felt justified and entitled to get the best from both his wives and was not concerned about how they felt in this miserable triangle that he had created. Even though Hansa held a special place for him, he felt that both women were duty-bound to follow his wishes and keep him happy. Any emotional outbursts or protests disturbed his peace and had to be dealt with firmly. Women needed to be shown their place. They were fed and clothed with a good house to live in, what more did they want? It was their inherent nature to crib.

Hansa and Nimmo tried to avoid each other as much as they could. Nimmo stayed in her room, and Hansa attempted to carry on with her routine as usual. Hukum Singh avoided interacting with Nimmo, except for stopping briefly to ask if she needed anything. Nimmo felt tortured each evening as she watched Hukum Singh and Hansa enter their bedroom and shut the door behind them. She felt like an intruder. The humiliation of being an unwanted guest in her own house was hard to bear. She wondered if she had taken the right decision in coming to Ambala for the delivery, but comforted herself that her child would be her ticket back into her husband's life. It was only a matter of a couple of months now, and her destiny would change.

Nimmo's mother had strongly advised her to use this opportunity to get back into Hukum Singh's life. "Men are fools," Chinti had said. "A woman has to manipulate and control her man who rules her destiny. A woman is physically weak, and her social standing comes from men. The only way she can control her life situation is to have a hold on her husband. For this, you must learn to use your youth, beauty and wiles at opportune times. Men are entitled to property, wealth and status they inherit from their fathers. Women inherit nothing; they must struggle to make and maintain a place for themselves. If you fail to learn the game of survival, you will remain a loser."

Nimmo was ashamed of her simple, ill-fitting clothes as compared to the stylish suits and saris that Hansa wore. She also observed how Hansa coiled her hair into a graceful bun at the nape of her neck and wore makeup. She compared her rough-skinned hands with Hansa's smooth ones with painted nails. Her dark feet with cracked heels seemed ungainly in front of Hansa's slender feet in buckled sandals. Nimmo was scheduled to go with Hukum Singh to the Military Hospital for a check-up. She wavered a long time between the four suits she had, all of which appeared equally shabby. On the way back from the hospital, she hesitatingly asked Hukum Singh if he could buy her a couple of new suits and sandals. Hukum Singh had himself felt embarrassed taking her to the hospital in rustic clothes. They stopped at the cantonment bazaar to shop and Nimmo looked to pick up the kind of clothes that Hansa wore.

"Call the tailor to stitch her suits, Hanso."

Hansa looked accusingly at him.

"Is there anything else I can do to serve your queen? You are so keen to dress her up prettily, why don't you go ahead and buy her some jewellery too?"

"Just control your tongue and stop nagging me."

Nimmo had been standing behind the door and heard it all. She came out and confronted Hansa with her eyes blazing.

"Just remember that you came here after me; you have snatched away everything from me, my home, my husband; and you still have the cheek to speak? Are you the only one who has a right to his earnings? Am I a servant in this house? Remember, I am his first wife."

"Don't you dare shout at me in my house; I will throw you out in a minute. If I have allowed you to come and live here, will you try to become the mistress? Remember your place."

"I have come to my husband's house, you witch, not yours. I have as much right to be here as you have. This is my child's house too."

Hukum Singh took Nimmo by the arm and propelled her out of the door.

"Shut up both of you. Don't create a circus here. I do not want to hear another sound from either of you. Go to your rooms and stay there."

Hukum Singh spoke aside to Hansa.

"Remember that she is carrying my child. A pregnant woman should not be put through any mental distress as it will affect the child too. She is uneducated. What is the use of your education if you cannot even understand that much? I do not want any more scenes in this house."

Nimmo tried to copy Hansa in her clothes and style. She stopped wearing a parandi, attempting to do up her hair in a bun. She dressed in smart suits ironed by the dhobi and no longer covered her head with a veil. Following the doctor's advice, she started to go out for walks in the evening. Hukum Singh received sizeable rations of eggs, butter, bread and meat from the army, so she got a wholesome diet. She also found the confidence to ask the khansamah to cook special dishes to satiate her pregnancy cravings.

Women from the neighbourhood had been itching with curiosity about the presence of an unknown, pregnant woman in Hukum Singh's house. A trail of enquiries led them to an old-time resident who remembered Nimmo from her earlier, brief stay with Hukum Singh. The knowledge that she was Hukum Singh's first wife created a lot of excited discussion and anticipation of drama within the women's group, and they decided to pay a visit to Hansa to get a closeup perspective of this interesting situation. Hansa knew there was no escape for her when she opened the door to three of her neighbours and ushered them into the drawing-room. She had barely seated them down and started making small talk when Nimmo walked in. She was nicely turned out, in her new blue, printed suit and net dupatta, her hair coiled in a bun. All eyes turned towards her for appraisal. She greeted the women and seated herself comfortably on a sofa.

Feigning ignorance, one neighbour looked questioningly at Hansa. "Is she your sister?"

Red in the face and trying to control a tremor in her voice, Hansa replied, "She is Nimmo behen, his first wife."

"Oh! That is why I was thinking, where have I seen her before? She looks so familiar. You were staying here earlier for some time, were you not?" she turned towards Nimmo.

"Yes, Behenji, I stayed here before Hansa behen came, and then I went to the village," replied Nimmo.

"Let me guess. You are in your seventh or eighth month. Am I right?" asked another one.

The women made enquiries about Nimmo's pregnancy, offered expert advice and were in no hurry to leave even after tea had been served. Hansa tried to cope with her embarrassment and had little to say; her social status and prestige had been blown to smithereens. It was now public knowledge that she was a second wife. Women would laugh and scoff at her. They would gloat over the fact that her co-wife was about to give birth to her husband's child while she remained barren.

As soon as Hansa had seen the women out, she countered Nimmo with a flaming face.

"Why are you bent upon insulting me in front of all my neighbours and friends here? Could you not have stayed in your room? Is it not enough that I have allowed you to come and stay in my house? Must you also make me the laughing stock of society? This story about my being the second wife will now be circulated all around, and people who respected me will snigger behind my back. Will that bring you great satisfaction? You are going to have a child. I am not. Is that not enough for you? How much more do you want to humiliate me?" She broke down crying and made to leave the room, but Nimmo blocked her way.

"So you think I have insulted you? I came to this house as a new bride with a heart full of aspirations and hope. I slept in the bed where you sleep now. The man you sleep with is my husband too. But I was thrown out like a discarded slipper to spend my days alone in the village serving his family like a slave. You cannot even imagine the kind of humiliations I have to go through every day. I may not be as pretty or educated as you are, but I have self-respect and honour. Hukum Singh and his family have violated my honour. I am an uneducated village woman; I do not how to move around in this society of sahibs. I do not know how to wear a sari or walk in high heels. Is that my fault? But Hukum Singh married me as I was and now I am going to be the mother of his child. Put yourself in my place and think how it feels to have been rejected for another. I have no other place to go. Since destiny has thrown us together, can we not live together like sisters?"

Hansa counselled herself to make peace with Nimmo. She realized that it was no use grudging her presence in the house. Even though she was given to natural petty jealousies and bouts of temper, Hansa was not a woman to nurture malice and hate for long. She was not unfeeling to the fact that Nimmo had been wronged too. Anyhow, she must accept Nimmo for the sake of her husband. It was only a matter of a couple of months, and Nimmo would go back to the village with her child. She started taking better care of Nimmo, getting fresh fruit for her and serving her extra milk and ghee. Nimmo, who had been initially wary of her, slowly came to relax and trust her. She also realized that she needed Hansa's support at this time, and it was in her interest to make peace. Both women started visiting the regimental gurudwara in the mornings and going to the park for evening walks.

"So you are hoping for a son? Have you thought of a name for him?" Hansa asked Nimmo.

"It is in Waheguru's hands, whether it is a son or daughter. But because he and Bebe want a son, I hope it is a son. I would like to call him Tara Singh," she said shyly. She had once asked Akhtar the meaning of his name, and he said it meant a star. "You are lucky to have studied up to college. I was very keen to study too, but Bapu ji was not ready to send me away from the village to study further. It would have changed my whole life. Maybe I would have had a better future if I were educated."

"I know how you feel Nimmo. It is strange how women have no say at all in choosing their destiny, becoming mere pawns in the hands of forces over which they have no control. But it is time they start getting educated and become capable of managing their lives."

"Promise me one thing. If something happens to me during childbirth, will you look upon and bring up my child as your own?" asked Nimmo.

"Why do you say so? Nothing will happen to you. Everything will be fine. Anyhow, I promise to look upon your child as my own," said Hansa.

Hukum Singh was surprised and much relieved to observe the friendship between the two women. He was excitedly awaiting the birth of his child.

17

Devil's Child

As the time for Nimmo's delivery came close, Jeeti came to Ambala for her grandchild's birth. She concluded her daily morning paath invoking Waheguru's blessings for a grandson. For the first time since Hansa's arrival in the family, her affections favoured Nimmo. She fussed around her, taking care of her diet and comfort. Nimmo's mother sent a tin of panjiri and asked if Nimmo could come home for her delivery, as was the custom. Jeeti refused, insisting that they would take no risks; Nimmo would deliver in the military hospital.

"See how your face glows. And I have noticed you crave more salty things than sweet. I am sure it's going to be a boy," Jeeti remarked.

Nimmo was all of twenty years of age and did not have the vaguest idea about childbirth. She felt increasingly anxious as her time drew near. Various doubts and fears flashed through her mind. Would it be a boy? How would the family react if it were a girl? Would the child survive and be normal? Would she survive the delivery? She recalled hearing about women dying during childbirth. She remembered her younger massi bearing much pain before bleeding to death during her delivery. Hukum Singh's uncle had lost two wives to childbirth and promptly remarried within a year each time. To add to it all, she did not have the security of a close and supportive relationship with her husband. If only she were back home with her mother and father. But she could not ask to go home—this was her only opportunity to make a comeback in Hukum Singh's life. Besdies, she could not risk the safety of her unborn child. Tense and restless, she lost appetite and often lay tossing around in her bed at night.

One day she saw a large brown owl perched on the parapet of her room window and was transfixed with terror as she looked into its large black eyes. It seemed to look down at her knowingly. Maji often said that owls look for devastation and howling dogs for death. She wanted to shout and shoo away this harbinger of bad luck, but her voice stuck in her dry throat, and she couldn't even manage a croak.

"Bebe ji, I am not well. Please call my mother. I don't know if I will survive this delivery. My heart keeps sinking all the time. An owl was sitting on the parapet of my window, and I had a bad dream early in the morning. I saw a black thief come and steal something from my house. He bit into it as he walked away, leaving behind a trail of blood. Maji says morning dreams usually come true." Nimmo broke down sobbing.

"Look at you blabbering on, girl! Don't bring such inauspicious words to your lips. Hai, hai, who has cast an evil eye on you? Do not worry; I will take care of it. May Waheguru keep a benevolent eye on us!" Jeeti drew closer to Nimmo and bent to whisper in her ear, "Do not accept anything white to eat from Hansa's hands like milk, kheer or curds. One can't say what childless women will do!"

A couple of dried red chillies were thrown on smouldering coals in an iron pan and circled around Nimmo's head seven times, the acrid smoke sending her into apoplectic fits of coughing. Bebe Jeeti had carried with her a kirpan brought from the holy Harmandir Sahib in Amritsar, which she slipped under Nimmo's pillow. It was a belief that iron should be kept close to expectant mothers for protection of the child from evil spirits.

Hansa noticed the change in Bebe Jeeti's attitude towards her ever since Nimmo had become pregnant. She became increasingly worried about her failure to conceive and consulted the lady doctor in the Military Hospital, who found nothing wrong with her. Come rain or storm—she went to the gurudwara regularly to pray for a child. Being a rationalist, she brushed aside any suggestions of miracle cures. She came to terms with the situation and was now looking forward to having a baby in the house. Even if she were not be the mother, it would be her husband's child. She was greatly pained when Jeeti tersely told her not to prepare Nimmo's food. She was well aware of the various superstitions and suspicions about childless women casting spells on pregnant women.

"Don't bother yourself with her food. I will see to it myself," Jeeti had said.

It was a wet, stormy night when Nimmo felt the labour pains coming on. It rained incessantly, and streaks of lightning and thunder ripped through inky skies with a malicious fury. Somewhere in the house an open window-pane banged wildly and broke a glass. The mango tree in the corner of the front lawn creaked and heaved as gusts of wind and rain lashed at it with demoniac force. A large branch ripped from the tree and landed in the lawn with a huge thud. Hukum Singh called for the ambulance and rushed her to the Army Hospital along with Jeeti.

It was a long wait as he paced up and down in the waiting lounge, while Jeeti sat turning prayer beads and reciting Gurbani paath. At last, her son would have someone to keep his name alive after him. What justice was it that Bachana, that boor of a man, should have two healthy children, while her moon-like son should have to beg destiny for a child. Hukum Singh, even though he would have prefered a son, had made peace with the probability of having a daughter too, as long he had a healthy child. It would deliver him from the terrible curse of being childless in a society that saw procreation as one of the major duties in a couple's life. It was said that a childless man's soul did not find deliverance even after death. The feeling of inadequacy for being unable to sire a child had eaten into his self-esteem. He was not to be blamed if the women he married turned out to be barren, but who could stop people from gossiping?

The smart Anglo-Indian nurse dressed in a white starched shirt and skirt, her stiff cap placed perfectly on her bobbed hair, walked out from the delivery room. Jeeti promptly got up and rushed to meet her.

"Is it a son? Is the baby healthy?"

"Congratulations! You have a healthy baby girl! It was a difficult delivery, but both the mother and the child are doing well. They have been shifted to their room, and you can come and meet them now," beamed the nurse.

Jeeti's face fell as she followed Hukum Singh and the nurse. "Whatever Waheguru wills. There will be a son next time," Jeeti consoled herself begrudgingly.

They walked through a long, spic-and-span corridor with white and green painted walls till she stopped in front of a room and opened its high, wiremeshed doors and ushered them inside. Hukum Singh adjusted his eyes to the semi-darkness in the room and saw Nimmo lying motionless with a white sheet drawn over her face; she looked eerily like a corpse. But when he looked at the crib, his heart beat faster with joyful anticipation as he peered down at the newborn baby swathed in a blanket. The nurse lifted her out of the crib and held her out to him with a broad smile.

"Go ahead and hold your daughter, sir!"

Hukum Singh extended his arms for the baby; then stopped in horror as he looked at her face. Jeeti stepped to take the baby from the nurse. She looked at the face of the baby and faltered, nearly losing her balance. The baby's small face lay starkly dark and ugly against the white blanket, a replica of Bachana's face. She had the same flat nose with a depressed bridge, prominent ears and a hare lip. The baby looked at Jeeti through dark, heavy lidded-eyes, screwed up her little face and let out a loud, lusty wail. Jeeti roughly laid her back in her cot and hit her forehead with her palm. Hukum Singh stood rooted to the ground. His mind could hardly accept what his eyes saw.

"This unchaste girl with a black face has smeared soot on our faces! May she not get a place even in hell!"

"Sir, your wife refuses to feed the baby. Please speak to her," a confused nurse addressed Hukum Singh. She did not follow Punjabi.

Both mother and son left the room without speaking to Nimmo. Perplexed, the nurse removed the sheet from Nimmo's face and spoke sternly.

"Madam, I understand that you and your family are disappointed by the birth of a daughter. But thank the Lord that both of you have survived a difficult birth. You both could have lost your lives but for the doctor's expertise. You are still young and will have more children. You must feed your baby."

"She is not my baby. She is the devil's child. Take her away. Why did you save us? I would have been better off dead. We should have both died." Nimmo whispered in a hopeless voice.

Nimmo had been weeping since she first set eyes on the baby girl and refused to hold her or feed her. It was clear as day that this baby was Bachana's progeny. She would have to pay for his lust. What would become of her now? Where would she go with her shame and fruit of sin? She would be accused of fornication and ostracised from the family, maybe even killed. No one would hear or believe her side of the story. Her dreams of regaining her husband's affections were smashed. She felt absolutely no maternal instincts for her baby, and the milk did not come to her breasts. Her soul seemed to have dried up as if the baby had sucked out the life from her. She found no answers to the various questions that hammered her mind. What would Hukum Singh do to her? Would he kill her? Would her parents take her back if she was thrown out?

Hansa opened the door to Hukum Singh and his mother.

"What's the news, Bebe ji? Is it a boy or a girl? Is Nimmo okay?"

Both walked past her without answering her.

"Is everything well?"

Hukum Singh, his clothes dripping wet from the rain, moved fast towards the wooden almirah in his room and started throwing out the clothes as he rummaged the shelves.

"What has come over you? What are you searching for?" asked Hansa alarmed.

"Where is my revolver?" thundered Hukum Singh. He was like a man possessed, and his eyes glinted maniacally. He continued to throw out the clothes and other things from one shelf after another.

"Hai rabba, what do you need your revolver for, ji? What has come over you? Please tell me what has happened," pleaded Hansa, trying to restrain him.

"I am going to shoot that deceitful woman of low birth and that bastard Bachana today. Find me my revolver now!" shouted Hukum Singh.

"Bebe ji, will you speak and tell me what the matter is? What has happened?"

"What should I tell you? Nimmo, the black-faced prostitute, has given birth to that bastard Bachana's daughter! Which self-respecting man can tolerate this? I wish the shameless hussy and her daughter had both died during childbirth! Hai rabba, I was blind not to see what was going on right under my nose. The shame that they have brought on this family! How shall we face the world when this scandal comes out!" lamented Bebe Jeeti.

Hukum Singh found his revolver, pushed the women aside and stormed out of the house even as they tried to restrain him. He was soon lost to them in the night leaving the wooden gate swinging after him in the whistling storm. He headed towards the hospital on the wet, empty road, till the discipline of years of military training returned, and sense overcame fury. It dawned on him that killing Nimmo would bring his career and life to an end, and that he could not escape the consequences of shooting her in the hospital with his service revolver.

He changed his direction towards the railway station. The platform was deserted as he sat down on a bench, unaware of his wet clothes dripping with rainwater. It was a few hours to morning, and the first train to Ludhiana would arrive soon. Bachana would answer to him. His brain numb with fury, he could not think beyond reaching the village and getting his hands on that bastard. He had defiled his wife, insulting him and hitting his honour in the worst possible way. He would pay with his life for it. That his wife had borne another man's child seemed to mock his own ability to father a child.

The hours seemed to stretch out as he sat waiting for the train, oblivious to his wet clothes. All this while, it never occurred to him that he had rejected Nimmo like an article he did not need any longer; that she may not have been a willing partner to Bachana's lust. He did not think of getting her version or giving her the benefit of the doubt.

That he could be responsible for inflicting the indignity and trauma of her violation did not cross his mind even once. That he was living with another woman after rejecting her was the most natural thing and entirely his right. A woman was a personal property, and responsible for guarding her pristine 'honour' as an obligation to her husband, family and society. Bachana's sin was not so much against Nimmo for sexual exploitation, but against his brother for defiling a woman who belonged to him. He bristled to think that she had been fornicating with Bachana and making a fool of him. He felt cheated and demeaned. He had been made a cuckold and would be mocked and laughed at by the entire world. How was he going to regain his honour?

It was daybreak and farmers were heading out to plough their fields when Hukum Singh reached his village house. The gate opened with a loud clang as he kicked it open. Bindo was sweeping the courtyard, and Amaro had just brought in a pail of fresh milk from the buffalo. They were taken aback to see Hukum Singh arrive dripping wet, with a frenzied look on his face.

"Where is Bachana?" he roared.

"What's wrong, Veere? Bapu ji!" Amaro stopped in her tracks and called for her father-in-law. Something was not right.

Sardar Naib Singh stepped out leisurely. He stopped in surprise when he saw Hukum Singh.

"Hukum, this is a sudden visit, is all well?"

"Where is that bastard Bachana?" Hukum Singh cut him short.

"He is not home. Calm down and tell me what is

wrong? Have you lost your senses?"

Hukum Singh rushed out without an answer and made for the fields. He saw Bachana standing by the well, instructing the fieldhand.

"You bastard, turn around and face me! Today you will meet your death. You shameless motherfucker!" he cried.

Stunned, Bachana turned around to face him.

"What do you mean? What has come over you?"

Hukum Singh fired the first shot in the air and pointed the revolver at him.

"You fornicator, you found no one else but your sister-in-law to blacken your face with? Even a devil spares seven houses!"

Taken aback, Bachana ran to take shelter behind a tree as the fieldhand sprinted towards the village, calling out to people for help. Sardar Naib Singh arrived and shouted for Hukum Singh to stop even as he fired several more shots one of which hit Bachana in the leg. The sound of gunshots and shouting by the field hand soon brought other men from the nearby fields to the scene. Hukum Singh was overpowered even as he struggled and continued to shout obscenities at Bachana. Someone tied up Bachana's bleeding leg and summoned a tonga to take him to hospital. Sardar Naib Singh and some villagers accompanied Bachana and waited for the bullet to be removed and the wound sewed up.

Bachana had lost much blood and lay pallid and unconscious—the doctor said that he would live but might lose his leg. He would have to stay in the hospital for a couple of days. Hukum Singh fled the scene. Villagers who had heard Hukum Singh abuse Bachana rushed back to the village to share it with others and soon everyone knew what the fight was about.

Back in Ambala, Hansa was trying to work out how to handle the situation. Jeeti declared that the bastard infant girl could not be allowed to live, and Nimmo must be sent back to her parents. She was worried that Hukum Singh had left the house with blood on his mind and was likely to do something rash, risking his job and safety.

"Go bring that prostitute and her spawn, and I will finish that fruit of sin with my own hands. No one will know. Newborn children die all the time. Nimmo can go and drown herself in some well or take poison if she has any shame," said Jeeti.

"I will not allow the murder of an innocent child in my home, Bebe ji. You should be more worried about your son right now. He left in a mad rage with a revolver in his hand. He will lose his job and go to jail if he does something violent. Our lives will be ruined. Go to the village immediately and manage the situation there."

Hansa put Jeeti on the first train to the village, and went to the hospital to meet Nimmo. The nurse told her that Nimmo had refused to eat anything or feed her baby. She had even removed the glucose that was being administered to her. The baby was on top feed, but they were concerned for Nimmo's health, who lay weak and spent, her face ashen against the white hospital sheets. Hansa sat down by Nimmo's bed and held her hand.

"Why do you refuse to eat, Nimmo? Your body needs strength now more than ever. Why do you refuse to feed the girl? Is there any mother who will not feed her baby?"

she asked.

"I do not want to live. Who will keep us? Hukum Singh will kill me anyhow. How can I feed this baby who has brought me so much shame? She is a curse to me. It's better for both of us to die. I can't face society with this blot on my forehead," said Nimmo.

"So what they say is true? Is she Bachana's baby?"

"Yes. But it's not my fault. I was forced to give in to him when he threatened and hit me. I did not dare tell anyone for the fear that I would be the one who would be blamed and kicked out of the house. No one wanted me there—Hukum Singh had rejected me, Bebe was already looking for an excuse to send me back home. I still have an unmarried sister. How could I go back and be an embarrassment to my parents and jeopardise her marriage? I could never imagine I would face such ruin." Nimmo broke down again.

"As a woman, I can understand what you have been through," said Hansa. "Fate can indeed play cruel tricks on us. Hukum Singh has sworn to finish you and Bebe will not let the child live. But you cannot give up. Be strong. We will have to think a way out."

"Let him finish both of us. There is nowhere I can go. My parents will not accept me with this child either. Maybe I should just take the child and jump into the river," sobbed Nimmo.

"You should never think of ending your life. Gurbani tells us that it is the gravest sin of all. The worst of situations have solutions, and you need to keep up your morale. Howsoever this child has come into this world she is innocent and deserves to live. I shall allow no one to harm her.

Give me some time, and I will think of what to do."

Hansa had Nimmo and her child discharged from the hospital.

18

Exodus

Jinnah's call for a separate nation for Muslims grew into a clamour, fanning fear and insecurity among communities. Aggressive reactions from Master Tara Singh and Hindu hardliners added fuel to the fire. Riots broke out all over Punjab; rumours about Hindu-Sikh massacres in West Punjab incited the hounding of Muslims in East Punjab. Faith divided neighbours who had lived together for generations in friendship and bonhomie. People hurried home before sunset and refused to open their doors to vistors who came knocking after dark, suspicious of each other even when crossing the street. Demonstrators marched through the streets shouting anti and pro-Pakistan slogans, and there were clashes between groups owing allegiance to the All India Muslim League, Indian National Congress and the Akali Dal, resulting in brick batting and street fights. Random stabbing incidents were reported now and then, even as mischief makers tried to provoke communal violence by throwing appendages of carcasses of cows in Hindu temples and pigs in mosques. Mysterious fires broke out in the dead of night gutting localities and reducing them to ghost streets of ash and rubble. Refugee trains—called 'Blood Trains'—pulled into Amritsar, carrying corpses instead of passengers, with blood oozing through their doors.

Sardar Naib Singh and Mian Ali Beg constituted a peace committee in the village and tried to calm down communal rage and suspicions among the people. But new rumours would erupt each day about alleged carnages somewhere and inflame passions again, leading to retaliation. Many leaders who lusted for power further aggravated communal feelings through incendiary speeches.

Mian and his family watched the deteriorating situation around them with alarm and trepidation. They had been confident that this disturbance was only temporary and would soon pass; things would return to normal sooner or later. There was no question of fleeing from their lands and home—how could one even think of abandoning a heritage handed down for generations? How does anyone think of relinquishing the only place one has known as home to become refugees in a strange land? The soil of their village was their identity and being, their fathers and forefathers having born and died there. Sixteen of their family members lay buried in their private graveyard on the periphery of the village. Mian Ali Beg was one of the leading and powerful men in the village and confident that he could hold his own with his two sons and retainers. He had a fair amount of arms and ammunition.

The Zaildar, having declared valiantly that no one could touch a hair on Mian's head as long as he was alive, indeed kept his word by coming to Mian's aid in repelling a hostile mob from a neighbouring village. The men had fired in the air, frightening away the mob armed with swords and axes. Criminal elements were making use of the chaos to get their hands on whatever they could loot; many were looking to lay their hands on women. Though the riotous mob was repelled, for the time being, it was not the end of the story.

They came again at night and took away several of Mian's cattle, kept in an enclosure a short distance from the haveli. One of the watchmen was cut down, while the other saved his life by hiding behind a stack of hay. There were rumours of Muslims being dragged from their homes, dowsed with kerosene and set on fire in the nearby city of Phagwara. Women had been raped and abducted. Hajjo pleaded with her husband and sons to leave for Lahore. More and more people were leaving each day, Sakina and her family had already left. They had Shammi's safety to think of.

Late one evening, after they had just finished dinner and laid out the cots in the courtyard, someone knocked at the door. Akhtar cautiously opened the door a little to check. It was his friend Kirpal Singh, a member of the Akali Dal, his face half-covered by the loose end of his turban.

"Akhtar my brother, I bring bad news—you are in grave danger. A huge armed group has planned to attack this village tomorrow to loot and kill Muslims. You have a young sister. I doubt that we will be able to protect you any longer. Please leave before the first light of the morning."

The family conferred with the Zaildar and decided that there was no choice but to leave. No one slept that night. A few things were hurriedly packed to be carried along. Early next morning before sunrise, Mian Ali Beg and his family went to say a tearful goodbye to the Zaildar and his family. The women hugged each other and wept as Mian Ali Beg handed over the keys of his haveli to the Zaildar. Shammi and Bholan said a tearful goodbye.

"I hand over my home and all it holds to you for safe custody, brother. We shall return soon after this madness dies down. I shall yet come and defeat you at chess. Stay safe. Rab rakha."

"Don't worry, brother. Your home and property will remain a sacred trust with me; I will guard it with my life. All this rioting will soon be over. Come back soon. Go safely. Rab rakha."

Packing for this tragic journey was an agonizing experience for Hajjo. Ali Beg had directed everyone to pack only essentials, as they had to hurry and could not carry much. He had heard that there were many murders merely to snatch away valuables from the people crossing over. Hajjo sobbed quietly, leaving all that she had put together so lovingly in the years since she came to this house as a bride. Silverware, beddings and kitchen utensils that she had brought in her trousseau would all be left behind in a moment. Her treasured Benarasi silk kurtas, chenille ghararas and lacy dupattas lay folded in her trunks, while her stores were stocked with grain and jaggery.

She packed a few clothes, and the holy Quran she read daily. She could not help slipping on a pair of bangles that had been in the family for three generations and handed down to her by her mother-in-law. She picked up a heavily embroidered phulkari embroidered by her mother for her trousseau, and then reluctantly placed it back. Then she picked up a silver water jug—she had quarrelled with her husband to buy it from Chaura Bazaar last Eid—wondering whether she could fit it in somewhere. Mian had carefully removed some bricks in an inner wall to hide their jewellery, hoping to retrieve it when they returned. She had to persuade a sobbing Shammi to leave behind most of her favourite salwar suits and trinkets.

Chinti gave Hajjo a cloth bag with eatables for the journey. As they were about to step out of the main outer door of the haveli , Mian Ali Beg and Hajjo looked back at their house for the one last time. Everything seemed just as it had each morning when they rose to start their day. A half-finished blue and white khes lay stretched on the handloom in the hall, with rolls of cotton thread in reed bowls next to it. The earthen chullahs were still warm with embers of last night's fire; the branches of the old neem tree in the courtyard swayed gently in the wind. The earthen oven had piles of firewood next to it, waiting to be kindled for the morning breakfast. String cots which had been slept in at night lay forlorn in the courtyard while washed clothes hung out to dry on a rope fluttered in the mild breeze. Hens clucked noisily in their pen in the corner of the courtyard. Ali Beg's pet white pigeons flew around the yard waiting for their feed. One of them alighted gently on his shoulder. Ali Beg could no longer fight the tears which streamed down his face.

"Oh, wait a minute, I forgot to lock the room upstairs,'

cried Hajjo, turning back.

"Let it be, begum, break your attachment with this home. No locks are going to keep it safe now. Allah knows whether we will ever set foot here again. Come, let's move, we have to meet up with the caravan in time," said Ali Baig in a broken voice.

"Hai, hai, Allah keep our house safe; please don't utter such inauspicious words. We shall definitely return soon."

Akhtar and Waseem had resisted the move for long. With the unshakable and brash confidence of youth, they could not imagine a situation they could not face. The boys had lived secure lives in a village where people had looked up to them for help and support. They were strong and had all the resources to safeguard their property. How could they allow some bigoted miscreants to displace them from their home and heritage? Akhtar had fought tooth and nail for an undivided India. The brothers tried to keep up brave faces as they saddled their horses.

The family's pet dog Sheru seemed to sense that something was not right. He ran behind Akhtar and started whining and barking as he mounted his horse. Unable to control his distress, Akhtar climbed down to pet the dog for one last time. His parents had moved forward in the rath meanwhile, calling out to him to follow. He hung back a little to gain composure and slowly trotted out of the outer courtyard, even as Sheru continued to bark and trail him. The dog persisted in following him out into the street and would not turn back. The first rays of the sun touched the still water in the village pond and lighted up the silhouettes of the onion domes of the gurudwara.

A veiled figure wrapped in a chadar stepped out from

the shadow of the gurudwara wall, waving a hand for him to stop. Akhtar was instantly on the alert and reached for the pistol in his waistband when a faint, familiar voice called out his name.

"Akhtar, stop. It's Nimmo."

Startled, he jumped down from his horse.

"What are you doing here at this hour? Are you all alone?"

"Yes, I am alone."

"Why? What has brought you here? Is everything well with you?"

"Nothing is well with me. I came here to take one last look at my home before I finish myself. God has been kind in granting me my last wish to meet you."

"Have you gone crazy? What are you saying? Tell me what happened?"

"I have nowhere to go. My husband will not keep me, and I know my parents won't accept me back either. There is no other option for me but to end my life."

"You should not say that. Even to think of suicide is haram. I heard you had a child. Where is she?"

"She is dead to me."

"This village is going to be attacked by rioters. It's not safe to stop here and talk. We are on our way to Lahore. Come with us, and tell me all about it later."

Nimmo looked back at the mud path that led to the old brick village gate and her parents' haveli. She thought of her mother, father and Bholan. Would she not be able to see them even once? Maybe this was best for all. How could she face them with her shame? Her mother would probably turn away her face, and her father might shoot her for dishonouring herself and the family. The rising sun bathed the village in a warm orange glow, and chirping birds started to fly out of their nests. Branches of tall sheesham and dark kikar trees swished in the gentle morning breeze. The sonorous voice of bhai ji reading out the morning verse from Guru Granth Sahib resounded in the morning stillness, alerting people to awaken for a new day. The muezzin's azan followed it to call out for Salat al-fajr, the early morning prayer. It would be her last memory as she mounted the rath and sped away from the village where she was born and bred, which had been the entire world to her for sixteen years. Sheru followed the rath till he was exhausted and could keep up no longer.

19

Journey to Lahore

Mian Ali Beg and his family set upon a perilous journey to Lahore, part of the fourteen million displaced people who crossed the border from both sides during the partition. The lucky ones made it across—upto two million lost their lives in this cataclysmic exodus. People had fled their homes and properties to an uncertain future and a lurking danger of looters, rape and violent death on the way. A violent exodus of such magnitude was a freak incidence in the history of mankind. Most victims of such a stupendous catastrophe were ill-prepared to deal with it emotionally and cognitively. There were no references to look back; neither had they seen nor heard anything like this from their ancestors. Gripped by intense fear, anger, loss, insecurity and helplessness, people were unable to find inner resources to cope with this onslaught, and many lost the cultural and moral values that regulate and direct an individual's behavioural choices. A complete breakdown of restraints and conscious filters gave way to wanton and destructive behaviour and mass hysteria. People lost the ability to think rationally. Age-old values handed down by religion and society crumbled in the face of a sweeping, communicable hysteria of hatred and violence pushing people into orgies of loot, arson, murder and rape.

Mian and his family joined a caravan of some twenty thousand evacuees, escorted by military personnel, crossing over on bullock carts, horses, raths, and on foot. They formed 25-miles long columns, with people carrying small children and bundles of belongings on their heads. The roads became clogged with men driving cattle, donkeys, sheep, and camels, raising clouds of dust. Trees flanking the roadside were stripped bare to feed animals and start fires to cook food, leaving behind a line of devastation, while the summer sun beat down hard on the travellers, exhausting them with heat and thirst. Terrified of stopping too often and eager to cross over to safety, they pushed on anyhow. When they stopped to rest after a long march, many old, ill and weak people collapsed from exhaustion, urging their family to move on without them. Animals dropped dead from hunger and fatigue. People groaned for the blisters on their feet and cried for water to wet their parched throats, causing a mad scramble for water wherever the column came across a pond or well. There was little to eat, and children constantly cried for food, their mothers begging those travelling by bullock carts and tongas to take them in. Mian Ali Beg took in two children in their rath.

A young man was carrying his aged father who could

walk no more, while his wife shouldered their four-year-old son. Pregnant with a second child, she too was on the point of exhaustion. The old man insisted that his son leave him behind and carry their child to safety. The young man put his father down by the roadside, hugged him with tears streaming down his face, lifted his son and walked on. An ill woman fainted and she was carried to a nearby sugarcane field and left to her fate, hidden in the tall crop. No one could risk slowing down and being isolated from the safety of the caravan. They crossed two caravans coming in from the opposite side, with equally devastated and ravished people. The countryside was dotted with many burnt buildings and fields, and one came across random human and animal corpses rotting on the roadside with vultures hovering over them. A young mother had stopped lactating due to stress and lack of food; her sickly baby who had breathed his last on the way due to illness and hunger was given a hurried, unceremonial burial by the roadside even as she wailed in low, keening sounds.

It took Mian Ali Beg and his family seven gruelling and traumatic days to cover a journey of two hundred and fifty kilometres between Sahnewal and Lahore. Evacuees were admitted to makeshift Transit Camps near the border, protected by army piquets, and were documented. Many people who had arrived with earlier caravans looked anxiously for relatives who had been left behind. A tent meant for ten people had thirty crammed into it for lack of shelter. It was tragic to see respectable people struggle and jostle to receive the paltry rations being doled out by the army.

Mian's family was one of the fortunate few who did

not have to stay in the overcrowded and disease ridden-camps. They were taken in by Sakina and her in-laws who owned a house in Lahore. Sakina could hardly believe her eyes when she saw Nimmo and hugged her with great affection. She could judge right away that something was very wrong. Exhausted beyond measure, all except Akhtar and Nimmo went to sleep soon after bathing and eating.

Nimmo borrowed Sakina's clothes to change into—it was a benumbing feeling to be in a strange place with not a person or a thing to call her own. But strangely, she felt no great fear or remorse. When one has been driven to the very end, to the point of having given up the wish to live, nothing causes further distress or pain. She did not know what her future would be like in this alien land, but she was relatively calm and resigned to meet whatever challenges she had to. She need not fear for her life any more—whatever happened, she was safe and would find a way to make a new beginning for herself.

After the family had eaten the evening meal, Akhtar summoned Nimmo to the rooftop. "I want to hear about all that has happened to you. You need not keep back anything from me."

Nimmo told him all about her unhappy marriage and Hukum Singh's taking a second wife. She narrated her miserable life at her in-laws, and the ill-treatment meted out to her. But she stuttered and stopped when she came to Bachana's exploitations, blushing with shame and humiliation.

"Do not think I will sit in judgement over you or hold you responsible for anything. I know you were a mere victim," Akhtar urged her on.

She mustered the courage to narrate her entire story and watched his face for reactions. Akhtar was quiet for a while, seeming to be in deep thought. Then he reached for Nimmo's hand and covered it with both his hands.

"I am shocked to hear about what you had to go through and pained that I was not in a position to do anything about it. I know you are in a state of fear and uncertainty about your future. I asked you to come along with us, so you are my responsibility now. Nimmo, I would like to marry you if you accept me. Can you leave your past behind and start a new life with me?"

Nimmo was too overwhelmed to say anything for a while, trying to control the tears streaming down her face.

"Will your parents agree?" she asked.

"There will be some reluctance, but I will convince them."

Akhtar and Nimmo were married by a simple nikah ceremony. Nimmo from Sahnewal, daughter of Zaildar Kehar Singh and wife of Major Hukum Singh of Raipur was reborn as Naaima Begum. Her past belonged to another era and another country, torn asunder by a ruthless destiny.

20

Tara

Hukum Singh's orderly passed him a pair of perfectly shined tan leather shoes as he dressed to leave for office. It was over a month since the baby's birth and his fight with Bachana. Nimmo was untraceable. Her parents were informed of the whole episode, but neither of the families made any efforts to trace her or the baby. Chinti and Bholan were the only ones who cried for her. Chinti was too scared to ask her enraged husband to look for her, and everyone came to believe that she had killed herself along with the baby. Hukum Singh's neighbours and friends were told that Nimmo and the baby had gone to the village.

***

Another loss hung heavy over Hukum Singh's mind. The partition of the country entailed division of the armed forces and equipment between the two dominions. By mid-August that year, the Army would divide into the Indian Army and the Pakistan army. Brother officers who had lived and fought together for a common land would be torn apart. Formations, units, assets, and indigenous personnel of the Army were all to be split, with two-thirds retained by the Union of India, and a third going to the new dominion of Pakistan. The Northern Command would go to Pakistan, while the Western and Eastern Commands to India. Most predominantly muslim units were to move to Pakistan. Though government employees serving in civil departments were free to join either dominion irrespective of their religion, those in the Defence Forces were denied this choice by the Partition Council.

On August 13, 1947, Hukum Singh's regiment hosted a grand banquet for the Muslims officers who were leaving for Pakistan. An air of deep pathos and incredulity overlaid the evening as officers sat drinking in the bar together, recounting battles in Burma and the North-East Frontier, and the shared celebrations and ordeals in a fraternity bound together by honour and commitment to the uniform. They raised a toast to the valiant battles fought together, and blood spilt to save a brother officer; the shared adventures of glorious hunts and jungle training; the sports trophies won together and the deep-rooted brotherhood which no partition could rip asunder. For the last time, they sat across the long mess table and shared shammi kebabs and caramel pudding, served in silverware engraved with regimental insignia. The regimental band played in the background. It was a poignant moment in history when the departing officers rose to say their farewells. Soldiers who had not flinched in the face of death spoke in voices trembling with emotion and could not hold back their tears. There was a round of wild Bhangra after the dinner to vent uncontainable emotions of pain, tragedy and the unbelievable turn in destiny, in the typical Punjabi spirit of countering all moments of joy or tragedy with gusto.

Captain Sadiq came and hugged Hukum Singh, handing him a small package.

"Sardar, this is the Sheaffer pen you lost to me in the horse races betting. Keep it till I come and win it again next year."

"Yara, what about our hearts that you are taking with you? I shall count the days for you to return for the next shikar season—we still have to nab that neelgai we lost," said Hukum Singh with a lump in his throat.

There was a feeling of painful incredibility to this tearing apart of a close-knit brotherhood forged with blood and a shared ethos, which had kept the Army unshaken and secular amidst the recent rioting and communal hatred blazing across Hindustan. The Army had been the only saviour in a volcano of hatred and violence, trying to maintain a semblance of order under grave risks. Many of them took the call of duty despite facing a threat to their families and properties. The Army took over driving and escorting trains to transport evacuees across the border, escorted huge columns of refugees crossing over on foot, managed transit camps for evacuees and rescued abducted women.

Ironically, the farewell party ended with the playing of the ceremonial march tune of the Armed forces—*Sare*

Jahan Se Achcha Hindustan Hamara—bringing down the curtain on centuries of a composite culture and brother-hood, torn apart for two identities forged in the cauldron of political ambitions, religious bigotry and British Machiavellianism.

***

Hukum Singh had been quiet and withdrawn, always refusing to discuss Nimmo's incident any further. Hansa sat beside Hukum Singh and took his hand in hers.

"There is something I must tell you. Do not be angry with me. I took Nimmo's baby from the hospital and kept her in an orphanage run by Christian nuns. I want us to adopt the baby as our own daughter and bring her home."

"How could you go and do something like this behind my back? I never want to look at that child's face again. Do you want to remind me of her betrayal and treachery each day I look at the child? I am glad she has gone and jumped into some well or river, and I did not need to wring her neck myself."

"You are a soldier and a protector sworn to lay down your life for saving those of others. How can you speak of taking someone's life? You judge her too harshly. Do you believe that it was she who betrayed you and not the other way round? Why do men think that they are the centre of the universe, and everything must be perceived in relation to their benefit? You are an educated man who should be able to look beyond the notions of patriarchy drilled into the collective social psyche. You married and abandoned a young, innocent girl because she did not come up to your expectations. But it was not her fault. She was who she was. She was abused and exploited by your brother, but you held her responsible. She put up with this humiliation because she was a rejected wife who had no options. She carried the onerous weight of the 'honour' of your family as well as her own on her young shoulders, and continued to suffer dishonour for it! I shudder to think about what she might have done to herself. She told me that she would take her life and I am afraid that she has drowned herself in some well or river. Hey Waheguru, I hope I am wrong. I cannot undo the wrongs done to her, but I will bring home and adopt her daughter as my own. It was my promise to her, and I must fulfil it. You must have realised by now that the problem of infertility did not lie with Nimmo or me—Nimmo was penalised for no fault of her own. The least you can do to repent is to give a home to her daughter. Children belong to whoever raises them."

Hansa brought home the baby and named her Tara.

Glossary

A note for the reader: For a period novel to be faithful to its times, use of vernacular words and expressions becomes inevitable, whose meaning may not always be apparent. Rather than litter page bottoms with footnotes, this glossary provides an easy reference.

achkan—long Indian men's jacket

ajwain—carom

angeethi—coal-burning clay oven

angrez—white people

ayah—nanny

baati—flat brass bowl commonly used in Punjab

bagge—of very fair skin colour

bahu—daughter-in-law

baithak—sitting room

bakhsheesh—tip

bal gopal—a son like baby Krishna

banjara—gipsy

bara memsahib—wife of a senior white officer

baraatis—members of a groom's wedding party

barkhurdar—son

behenji—elder sister

bhabi—brother's wife

bhatti—fire pit for cooking

bhishti—water carrier

biradari—community

boori—a blonde buffalo

chadar—an outer veil worn by women

chamar—an erstwhile untouchable community

cheent—a printed cotton fabric of yesteryears

chullah—clay oven

dai—midwife

dandal—epilepsy fit

dargah—muslim place of worship

degh—cooking vessel

devi—goddess; also a way of addressing women

dhobi—washerman

doli—vehicle carrying a bride after her wedding

dozakh—hell

dupatta—ladies veil

dushehra—Hindu festival commemorating Lord Rama's victory over King Ravana

fauji—army man

ganga mai—mother Ganges (river)

geete—game of five pebbles

ghagra—heavily pleated long outer skirt worn by women

gharara—ladies trousers pleated at the knees

ghat—shore

giddha—punjabi folk dance for women

git-mit—confusing babble in english

gota jaal—heavy embroidery in shining lace

guluband—choker necklace

gusul—bath

halwa—a sweet made of flour, butter and sugar

halwai—cook and sweet maker

hanji—yes

haram—forbidden by religion

haramzaadi—bastard woman

haramzada—bastard

hoori—celestial beauty

hoorpari—beautiful celestial woman

isai—christian

jagir—land received from rulers in lieu of services

jagirdar—owner of large landholdings

jalse—festivals

jattis—Jat women

jemadar—sweeper

jemadar—cleaner

kaka ji—a respectful way to address young men

kalgi—aigrette

kalyug—the age of sin in hindu mythology

kanjari—dancing girl

kantha—neck ornament for men

kara—steel bangle worn by sikhs as a religious symbol

karah parshad—sweet distributed in the gurudwara

khala—muslim name for mother's sister

khalsa—baptised sikhs created by Guru Gobind Singh

khandan—extended family

khansamah—cook

khes—hand-woven cotton duvet

khussa—embroidered punjabi footwear with an up-turned toe

kimkhwab—an expensive, rich woven fabric

kirpan—dagger carried by sikhs as a religious symbol

kothri—store

lacha—a loose cloth tied at the waist by men

lachchami—Lakshmi, the hindu goddess of wealth

laddoo—sweet made from chickpea flour

laften—lieutenant

langar—community kitchen

lassi—churned whey drink

lehriya—cloth with diagonal stripes

madrassa—traditional muslim school

mai-baap—mother and father

makkaan—visit by relatives to offer condolences

mali—gardener

malik—owner

mannat—wish

mantar—religious spell

massaya—moonless night with a supernatural aura

mazar—tomb of a muslim saint

memsahib—white woman

mirasan—muslim community of minstrels and entertainers

mul-mul—fine muslin fabric

murkian—small round earrings worn by men

navratras—nine days for worshipping hindu goddess Kali

paath—recitation of sikh hymns

panjiri—sweet mixture of roasted flour, ghee and nuts

paronthe—fried wheat-flour pancakes

patasas—sugar candies

peehri—low sitting stool woven in cotton cord

peer—muslim saint

phulkari—veil embroidered in a traditional punjabi design

pinni—a traditional punjabi sweet made of butter, flour and sugar pippal patti jhumkas—punjabi design for earrings

poore—sweet pancakes

puja—hindu prayer

punkah—fan

rakhri—a festival when sisters felicitate their brothers

rathwan—driver of a rath

red mauli—red cotton thread supposed to be auspicious

roti—wheat pancake

rudraksh mala—necklace made of dried rudraksh fruit, held to be holy

saag—popular punjabi leaf vegetable

salu—red dupatta worn by a punjabi bride

sandook—wooden boxes

sanjog—pre-destined to meet

sarwan—a legendary son highly devoted to his parents

sattu—barley drink

sayaana—shaman

sewian—flour noodles

shagun—gift money given on auspicious occasions

shani—mythological hindu deity

shia—an islamic sect

shloka—a verse from the vedas

siapa—dirge

stapu—game of hopscotch

suhagan—married woman

tagma—medal

tai—wife of father's elder brother

tandoori chicken—roasted chicken

tatti—reed curtain to keep out the heat

taveet—talisman given by a shaman

thaat-baat—glamour

tikka—decorative religious mark on the forehead

tola—measure of weight (usually for gold)

tonga—horse driven carriage

vilayat—England / Britain

vilayati—English / British

zamindar—land-owning farmer

.